A Love Affair with a Billionaire

ANANDA JOY

A Love Affair With A Billionaire
Copyright © 2023 by Ananda Joy

Printed in the United States of America.

ISBN
979-8-88945-327-7 (Paperback)
979-8-88945-328-4 (eBook)
979-8-88945-329-1 (Hardback)

Brilliant Books Literary
137 Forest Park Lane Thomasville
North Carolina 27360 USA

Table of Contents

Life

Sometimes a person enters your life when you least expect it, someone who at the time you didn't realize was so important. Someone who you only later recognize what an angel, what a gift, what a miracle this person was in your life. Once they are gone you are not the same, nothing is the same and their impact lives forever in every moment of your life, in every breath that you take, in every thought you think. You know that you would never take one moment back, yet you wished you had seized more moments while they were there to take.

If I had a few moments to be with him again, I would hold him tight in my arms and let him know how much I love him, how much I appreciate him. I would pour out my gratitude for how he loved me so purely, so absolutely, so perfectly. I would tell him how deeply, profoundly, and completely I love him and will continue to love him for all eternity. I would tell him that he has saved me in a million ways and I will never know how to repay him... that there will never be a moment when I am not deeply grateful to him. I would tell him that he is perfect and beautiful and the most fascinating man that ever existed. I would thank him a million times for blessing me with his gift of love, joy, creativity, inspiration, and his example of a man who loves without limit. I would thank him for all the little things and all the big things but most of all for being himself... for sharing his love so generously... for sharing his unique and extraordinary human expression.

I would apologize for all the times I took him for granted, for the times I got upset and misunderstood him or projected my own confusion onto him. For the moments I wasn't fully present to him, for the times I wanted something from him rather than just being with him. I would really look at him, be with him with no agenda, just to be fully present to and enjoy the magnificence of his soul expression through the physical identity Matthew.

I traveled over 2,000 miles to a new town with barely any money, two kids under four, no car, no job, and no family… only two friends I barely knew. I began working for a very low wage at my children's daycare… not because I didn't have a college degree, but so I wouldn't be away from their tender hearts all day long… how I made it on my measly income I will never know. As my children grew and began attending public school I worked in the public school system and later became a massage therapist and built my own very successful private practice.

Angels were there to help me and conspire events that would bring me to the people I needed to meet and the opportunities I was blessed to enjoy. I met a woman who came to the student massage clinic while I was in school, and I was *randomly* or more accurately synchronistically assigned to be her massage therapist. She began requesting me to be her massage therapist and we began developing a beautiful friendship. She is a very talented healer and life coach and she was looking for someone to share her office space… she offered me the opportunity to share the space with her for massage trade. I was very grateful and felt honored to accept this blessing… she was my angel. It was perfect how the universe conspired through the loving generosity of my new angel friend to arrange that opportunity for me to begin my practice with no upfront money. I purchased a used table from the school and a couple pairs of sheets and I was in business.

It was a learning curve at first, I learned quickly where to put ads and more importantly where *not* to put ads, and I became quite competent at screening clients over the phone to keep my clientele honest and delightful people who were seeking massage for therapeutic purposes only. My favorite clients were those who were referred by my clients… it was always a joy to meet my client's friends and loved ones. My clients became my friends and that is how I began building a friendship base in this new town. I also attended and taught my own classes on meditation, spirituality, healing, and energy work and developed many new friendships that way.

It is interesting how events in our lives that seem so unimportant and insignificant can be pivotal in leading us down a whole new path and adventure that transforms our lives completely. One day I felt guided to go to a friend's Sunday meditation. After the meditation one of the people attending purchased a massage gift certificate from me for his girlfriend. It was not unusual for me to sell gift certificates, especially on holidays and for birthday or anniversary gifts… however looking back at the very moment I listened to my guidance to go to the meditation and as I follow the thread of events, I realize it led me to the most amazing adventures of my life. I went to the meditation… someone purchased a gift certificate… he gave the gift certificate to his girlfriend… who became a regular client… and she recommended me to a friend who became a very unique client who would change my life forever.

Two weeks after the completion of an abundance course I taught in my home this very unique client came for a massage.

A New Client

It was just like any other typical day, my schedule was fully booked but I always left a short amount of time to sit in meditation while waiting for my next client. In a burst of energy, a very spry, handsome, and energetic man bounded into my office with a huge smile on his face. His boundless energy practically knocked me over. He had books in his arms and took control right away with conversation and questions. To this day I wish I was relaxed enough to flow with this divine moment… flow with his energy and find out all about what books he had brought and allowed him to control the time.

However, I was on a schedule and had another client after him and became directed to get things moving… so I did the usual rigid routine of signing paperwork and leaving the room so he could get under the sheets for his massage. I was living life in survival mode… my mind very fixed and directed. There was little room for spontaneous outbursts into the unknown… everything was very structured. I alone had to feed my two children and keep a roof over their heads, and that was my main focus.

I forgive that frightened self I used to be… I understand her and love and appreciate her… I know that she was doing her very best. When I look back she amazes me… how she had the courage to leave an abusive relationship, move across the country far away from all her loved ones to a new and strange town to start a new life for her two children and herself. I look at this 31-year old woman who came into this new town with one suitcase, no job, no car, no friends, no babysitter, maybe a thousand dollars and two hungry toddlers.

I see how she used the power within her soul to build a life from almost nothing. She made many, many friends, built a very successful business, became a minister and created a non-profit organization that offered spiritual classes, regular meditations, trainings, and supported charities world-wide.

Raising my children alone was never easy… but always my first priority. I was grateful for the secondhand stores where I was able to get all their cloths, bikes, toys, and everything we needed at a very low price. As things got better and business picked up they soon had all the things all the other kids had, and we lived a good life.

I was never someone that could fit in the mold of the traditional world, I always had to do things my way, and even though they were unorthodox, life always seemed to work out surprisingly wonderful. It wasn't as if I was seeking out miracles… I just went about my life, following my heart, doing the very best I could and synchronicity found me.

I look back in wonder at the woman I was, working sixty hours a week, holding community meditations, teaching classes, and volunteering in the community while raising my children alone. I was a committed mother… helping out in their classrooms… making it to every recital, performance, field trip, baseball, and football practice and game. Who all alone without any help came home and ran the kids to their practices, helped with homework, did the laundry, made dinner, kept the house and yard clean, and still had time for hide and seek tickle. I honor her because I couldn't be who I am today without her, and I love who I am today.

This wonderful new client was Matthew and he was one of my older clients, but when I asked him if he had any concerns or pain he said with a jolly laugh "Oh no, not at all, I feel wonderful". I had people in their twenties coming in with lists of complaints and here this man in his seventies feels like a million bucks. I knew in that moment that Matthew was different… he was unique and special… I just didn't know how much. When he told me his age I was surprised… he had seemed so much younger. He had a full head of neatly combed red wavy hair… he was slim, energetic, and fit… and he had an attractive unwrinkled face. He told me how he played racquetball, jogged, and did sit-ups everyday. He was the sexiest, most handsome, youngest looking man in his seventies that I had ever seen.

He left me a book of poems he had written. I was glad I took the time to read the poems because somewhere in the middle of the book he had hidden a one hundred dollar bill. I realized later that he loved to do little surprises like that… it was a part of who he was. I called him up right away and told him that his next massage was paid for.

Matthew became a regular client and I began looking forward to his appointments because we talked and laughed and shared so much… he was like the most comfortable friend… like being with myself yet not alone. He suggested one day that I come to his home to give him a massage and I agreed, however I informed him that I charged double for home visits because in the time it took me to do a home visit I could do two massages in my office. He was totally ok with paying extra so we made a date.

When I knocked on his door it seemed he was standing there waiting for me… within seconds he opened the door with a smile as big as life itself. He gave me a giant hug that matched his giant smile… I felt embraced by an angel. It was much more fun meeting Matthew at his home for massage… he was more himself in his environment… even more jovial, which I didn't think was possible. He was so thoughtful in that he would always have a carefully designed table display when I came. He had a very creative mind, so it was always different but usually included a cute note, some flowers, trinkets, money, and often a picture he had drawn or poem he had written. Sometimes he had books, photos, information or paraphernalia he wanted to share or talk about… it was always done creatively and artistically with thoughtfulness and care… it was an expression of his love and his immense spirit.

The Shift

When I first started coming to his home for massage I would feel anxious and want to leave right away after his massage, but over time something happened and I lingered longer and longer after the massages. We would talk, laugh, share stories, sip tea together, and look out at the mountains. It became more and more comfortable, easy, and relaxed and soon I hated to leave.

I remember one day after a massage and some visiting, Matthew invited me to a late lunch at a Chinese restaurant. I had plans to meet my boyfriend later on that evening but there was plenty of time to have a meal with Matthew and still meet my boyfriend… so I accepted. I didn't know it at the time but this may have been our first date. It was so much fun, we sat on the floor in a private room and enjoyed a wonderful meal and one another's company. As our meal was winding down Matthew told the waiter to hurry with the check… that I needed to meet my boyfriend. I was surprised because I hadn't peeped a word that I was meeting my boyfriend later. Matthew was like that though… sometimes he just knew things… he was so intuitive it was almost scary.

I guess I was completely naive because I hadn't realized that his love and affection for me had moved from friendship to romantic love. I deeply loved the man I was dating at that time, but we had broken up a few times and my heart was unsure if it was a forever type of love. I've learned so much since then, and realize now that all love is forever and no love is forever… but whatever love you have right now is the perfect love… for right now.

However, my mind couldn't imagine a romantic love with Matthew because of our age difference and I was really looking for that one true soul mate I could marry and run off into the sunset with. I was so caught up in a future fantasy I wasn't fully present to the magic, love, passion and beauty that was unfolding in present time.

My boyfriend Philip and I had a very deep connection and love… however there had always been a lot of fear around dating him. Sometimes for no reason when we were together I would get anxious and feel doubts about the relationship. It got confusing at times because although there were doubts and fears, there was also a very deep connection and love, a dear friendship, and great sexual chemistry. I was puzzled that I felt I could be more myself with Matthew than with Philip, but there was more attraction and chemistry with Philip… at least in the beginning. So I continued to date Philip and kept Matthew informed that I had a boyfriend.

Philip was a little uneasy with me becoming friends with this new older man, but he never gave me a hard time and never asked me to not hang out with him. Philip and I had a mature relationship, we didn't feel the need to control one another or get upset about much. We enjoyed things like camping, motorcycle rides, walking, and talking… it was a down to earth and friendly relationship.

What I hadn't realized at the time was that my mind and my heart were having a battle and that my heart would of course win out. One day as I was listening to one of Matthews always amusing voice messages on my phone, I felt my heart pang and I felt tingly and warm all over. I was confused… how could I feel this way about this man who was twice my age? I of course brushed those feelings off, but they did get my attention and I've never forgotten that moment.

One day when I was giving Matthew a massage I had a vision of the two of us just lying on the bed with all our clothes on… holding one another as intimate friends, merging our energies and becoming one. It was compelling and strong, yet I disregarded it as a crazy thought.

The Sacred Cabin

One of the most sacred days of our relationship was the journey to the mountains. He said he wanted me to give him a massage at a different place… that he would drive us there and that we would need much more time than usual. So we drove up towards the mountains, turned onto a windy dirt road and ended at a dead end at the top of a hill where a lone cabin sat. He stopped the car and said that we were here. He bounced out of the car with a big smile and began bounding toward the cabin… a simple little cabin in the woods.

The house was a rosy, chestnut color with a tin roof… it looked very old yet very quaint and charming. It was nestled amongst pines and aspens with a sweet little brook that passed right in front of the house. I followed him… I was curious as to what he was preparing to show me. He opened the door to the cabin and invited me in. He opened the blinds of every window, turned up the heat, and turned on a couple lights. He then proceeded to head toward a big bucket and he scooped out a big handful of peanuts. He looked at me, smiled, and said, "Follow me"… he went out onto the back porch and proceeded to put peanuts on the deck railing an inch or two apart. As soon as he was a few feet away from the first few peanuts a big blue jay snatched up a peanut, and soon thereafter a squirrel got into the action. The entertainment far exceeded the cost of the peanuts.

Matthew was in his glory, beaming with joy as he continued to gift the creatures of the woods handfuls of peanuts that got snatched up almost as quickly as he put them on the railing. I had to laugh, it was the best entertainment I had had in a while, and out in the woods with the pines and aspens… that beautiful smell of the high country… I was in heaven.

We went back into the cabin and he proceeded to show me around the palace. He told me how a group of men who were working for him had stolen a large amount of construction materials from him. Matthew never turned them in to the police… he simply turned the other cheek. These men were so touched by his good nature that they remodeled his old trappers cabin as payback for what they stole from him and to acknowledge his kindness of not pressing charges.

He told me how he acquired the property… how he and two other men were looking to purchase the land together… they split the property into three parcels. He knew immediately which piece he wanted… he loved the piece where the old broken down trappers cabin resided… but he didn't give away his excitement. He downplayed the spot and let them both choose first… luckily for him they choose the other spots and he was "left" with the broken down trappers cabin.

As Matthew began showing me around the small cabin he led me into a bathroom off the kitchen, and to my surprise the bathroom led into another bathroom, which led into a big master bedroom. As he took me through this secret hidden addition to the cabin I had a profound deja vu. It was such a powerful deja vu, that I had to sit on the bed a few moments because I felt a bit dizzy and disoriented. I was surprised and had not expected to see this secret room behind the bathroom. It had a hot tub, a massage table, high ceilings with lots of windows and a door to the outside deck. It was decorated with darling little trinkets, candles of all shapes and sizes, and there were several stuffed animals up on a shelf. I could see that outside the windows there was a bird feeder that had fallen on the ground and appeared broken. I could see the forest with trees of all shapes and sizes and when he opened the back door I could vaguely hear the little creek that passed in front of the house. It all seemed so magical and beautiful... somewhat surreal.

Matthew had the day planned and next on the agenda was a walk. Matthew was in good shape... I tried to keep up with him on the snow packed trail as he led us up a big hill... I was huffing and puffing. I thought what amazing shape he was in being in his seventies and not even breathing heavy... I'm in my thirties and getting out of breath. Once we got up the hill things were a bit easier and we enjoyed the quiet pristine winter woods together. As we travelled back on a twisty trail that followed a stream there was a squirrel squawking, and many little winter birds busily chirping and looking for food. It was a beautiful change from normal life in the city... not what I was expecting that winter day, but so very welcomed and appreciated.

It was nice to get inside the old cabin that was all warmed up by now and glowing with life force and energy. It was time now for me to give Matthew a massage. I will never forget this massage... it was my favorite massage I ever gave him. We had all the candles lit and he put on some music. I don't know if it was the music that was playing, the ambiance of the cabin, or the energy of our souls merging... however during the entire massage I felt sexy, erotic feelings flowing through me and they felt so sensual and natural I didn't repress them in the slightest. I just let them pass through me and delighted in feeling the bliss of being a sensual woman. I never told him how I felt during that first massage at the sacred cabin, but I believe that I received more enjoyment from that massage than he did.

After the massage Matthew asked me if I wanted to cuddle. I was a bit surprised and hadn't expected this twist in the day, but I said yes because I love to cuddle and in my mind I had pictured us fully clothed sitting on the couch snuggled up to one another enjoying the view of the snow capped peaks out the living room window. Matthew promptly began pulling the blankets down on the bed and asking if I wanted to take my jeans off to be more comfortable. I was taken aback for a moment and said that I didn't think we were going to cuddle in the bed. He said with his confident assuring voice, "Nothing is going to happen and you can leave your jeans on… the bed is just the most comfortable place to cuddle." He had a point, so I kept all my clothes on and jumped into bed with him and we snuggled and talked a few minutes and then just rested. I fell asleep at some point, but when I awoke it didn't feel like the usual sleep, it felt different, it felt like somehow I was transformed or healed… that something within me shifted in a really wonderful way.

Later we had lunch by the fire, Matthew would get up occasionally to throw another log on or stoke the fire and then return with a proud smile. This was one of the most magical days of my life, but what I hadn't known at the time was that there would be many more magical days at the cabin, and each one was like a link in the chain of a long magical adventure. I realized as I drove home from that visit that the vision I had a week ago had materialized without me doing a thing to resist it or push it happen.

Saturday Night

$\mathcal{W}$e began meeting at Matthews home every Thursday for his massage… the massage appointment gradually expanded to half or all day long. We enjoyed one another's company so much that time seemed to fly by… our visits never felt long enough. As time went on and we enjoyed sharing meals, sunsets, energy, thoughts, creativity, concerns, and ideas... we also began snuggling together in bed almost every time we visited. The more we snuggled it seemed the less clothes we wore until I was down to my underwear and bra. It was different when we snuggled and could connect skin-to-skin… we would hold and squeeze one another, we would hug, caress, and spoon. It was more intimate… it was an energetic delight how our soul energies would merge and expand into rapture without ever even having sex. It was so beautiful I imagined one time if what we experienced could be put into art it would be an exquisite masterpiece inconceivable to anything I've ever seen in form. I felt one with Matthew, I felt safe and loved like I had never before felt. There was an ecstasy when our energies merged… there was an ecstatic experience of knowing that there was only one of us.

With every visit we became more connected, we sat closer, held one another tighter and it seemed impossible not to have our hands touching the other… even if it was just to caress one another's arm or leg. It was like both of our energies expanded when we were together… like we were one huge very delicious energy field. Our hearts filled with ecstasy every time we became immersed in our shared ever-expanding energy field. I began to feel him even as I separated physically and drove home to take the kids to dance and football… do the laundry and cook dinner. We began calling every night to connect and bask in that shared energy and profound love… each night as we went off to sleep we were cradled in the blissful warm glow of our shared energy field.

I had worked Saturday evenings and all day Sunday's since I started my business, so I had not had a Saturday night off in a few years. I've never been one to party or go to clubs so it never bothered me… I was very content to spend my free time with my children and Matthew. During one of our visits, Matthew invited me to come over to his home on Saturday night to just hang out… no massage, no sex, just a fun evening together. My first reaction was no I have to work… but Matthew had a way of charming me and he sweet-talked me into it.

I had a concern though… by this time I had broken up with Philip but I knew that Matthew was married. I wanted to know more about Matthew's wife… I thought it was important to get the whole wife thing straightened out because we hadn't really talked about it other than he was legally separated from his wife. I never saw Matthew with a wedding ring on and he never mentioned his wife other than telling me he was separated. They obviously lived apart because of all the many times I had visited his home no one was around but he and I. Only his clothing hung in the bedroom closet, only his things in the bathroom, there was no sign of a female living in his house whatsoever.

So I asked him to tell me more about his wife, their relationship, and where she lived? He said that she lived in a nursing home, that they have been legally separated for years, that they haven't had sex since the early sixties, and that they live completely different lives.

This information was reassuring to my mind, but of course I wondered why they didn't just get a divorce. Matthew said it was for their children, and due to political and religious pressures. Being the free spirit that I am I didn't completely understand… I couldn't imagine not being free to follow my heart and live my highest truth in all that I do. In many ways I was freer than Matthew to live my life authentically where he felt very pressured by external forces to live by external rules and obligation.

It felt strange as I got into my car to drive over to see Matthew that Saturday night because I hadn't had a Saturday night off from work in a few years. When I got to Matthew's house he greeted me with one of his great big smiles and led me into the kitchen where he had flowers, a card, a bottle of wine, and some cheese and crackers all displayed in an creative and artful way on the kitchen countertop. What a beautiful sight it all was, but the most beautiful sight was his big warm smile as he glowed with pride.

We started with the wine and cheese and because I rarely drank it didn't take long for me to feel a bit tingly and warm from the alcohol. We had so much fun talking and laughing… I learned many new things about Matthew that night that I hadn't know… we discovered some synchronicities that surprised us. I learned that Matthew had studied A Course In Miracles… a spiritual study I had also studied since the late 1970's. It is a small world… he told me how a woman he previously dated had introduced him to "the Course" and they had gone to many meetings and gatherings together with people I had known. We actually had some mutual friends. He also had gone to the Science of Mind church and the local drum circle at the town park… we were both sure we had been to many of the same New Age spiritual and social events over the years.

We realized we had a lot more in common than we knew. We were having such a great time in conversation…sharing ideas and telling stories… time just flew by. At some point Matthew put on some music and we began to dance, he twirled me around the room and held me tight and then spun me around again. I couldn't stop laughing and couldn't remember a time I had had so much fun. It was all so exhilarating and definitely a night I would never forget

Becoming fast friends

As time went by we began to spend more and more time together, we talked on the phone several times a day and we enjoyed the connection so much that if too much time passed without connecting in some way we felt strange. Matthew participated in my life more and more, and we became fast friends. I had Matthew over for dinner occasionally and he and my children got along wonderfully. He was the type to meet children at their level and make them feel comfortable and at ease.

One beautiful sunny day he invited the kids and I to his cabin in the woods and we all had the time of our lives. When we got there he had these kits for the children to make an eternal handprint mold… he also had bubbles and some toys. I thought that was so thoughtful of him, and we will always cherish those ceramic handprints. Matthew drove the children and I up the mountain in his car and let them put their heads out the sunroof. When we got to the top of the hill we spent an hour or so playing games and horsing around. When we came down from the mountain we had a delicious dinner out on the deck as we watched the sun set and the creatures preform for us as they competed for the peanuts.

We began meeting up at the cabin on weekends every now and then, sometimes with the children and sometimes just the two of us. One time when the children and I met him up at the cabin it was wintertime so we hung out inside most of the day. We played a charade type of board game and Matthew had to act out the word "relieved." It still makes me laugh when I picture Matthew being such a good sport with the kids and I. He got up and acted out a hilarious animation of pretending to go to the bathroom… we were all in stiches laughing… he had an amazing sense of humor. We all have many found and dear memories of hanging out at the cabin with Matthew.

I remember the first time I came to Matthew's home to give him a massage, it was October and he played Christmas music. At the time it seemed too early to be listening to Christmas music, but he is the client and whatever music he wants is ok with me. In no time winter and the holidays had arrived and he often played that same Christmas cd… it seemed to be his favorite and it still reminds me so intensely of him. The holidays were so full of joy, it was such a special time for a new and wonderful relationship filled with constant surprises and new experiences. His first surprise and first real gift to me was a new massage table. I had purchased a used table for my massage business and it wasn't the real cushy soft plush type of table… it was all I could afford at the time. He noticed how I liked his massage table at his home and in his cabin in the woods and so he surprised me with the exact same table for my birthday that year. He had it delivered to my home and it came right on my birthday. It was the best birthday gift ever!

That Christmas Matthew gave me the best Christmas gift… better than anything I could have imagined. It was my year to have the children for Christmas Eve, and Christmas morning and so at around two in the afternoon they went to spend Christmas day with their father. When I got home from dropping them off at their dad's I felt so let down and lonely. I cleaned up the mess of wrapping paper and toys that were scattered about and made myself a little dinner and sat on the couch to watch the tree glisten on Christmas night. I called Matthew and he was with his children and grandchildren, and talking to him helped me feel better, but when we hung up I felt alone again. I felt so down I just put my plate on the floor and pulled a blanket over me and fell asleep on the couch listening to the same cd play over and over because I had put it on repeat and was too lazy to turn it off.

Around 5 am the next morning I heard the back door slide open and I looked up to see Matthew's beaming smile. He had come over with some very fattening pastries and all the love a heart can hold. He came into the living room and snuggled under the blanket with me and we lay there together for a couple hours in silence listening to the same cd repeat over and over. Just having him there took all my loneliness away and healed my heart. I felt surrounded in so much love and joy I couldn't wipe the smile off my face. I felt so loved by Matthew… fully embraced by his loving heart and powerful soul energy. I felt so intimate with him just laying there, holding one another, him in his pajamas and me still in my clothes but there seemed nothing between us, like we had merged into one person, one vast energy field… one loving presence. We eventually got up from the couch turned off the music and had a delicious pastry breakfast together. His early morning visit was the best Christmas gift I had ever received.

Passion

*W*e began spending almost every Saturday night together as well as all day Thursday and often whenever else we could connect during the week. Saturdays became very special… the two of us fully enjoyed basking in one another's company. Matthew would always make the evening an adventure even though we never left the neighborhood. Every Saturday night after a meal, a couple drinks, maybe a walk and always some dancing and laughing we would end up in bed snuggling and holding one another however we hadn't crossed that line of making love.

I was driving to meet Matthew on a beautiful Saturday afternoon… as I drove across the valley I enjoyed the awakening of life force all around me. Light green baby leaves were budding out from the brown branches of the trees… flowers of all shapes and colors were smiling at me, and the birds were joyously singing and dancing filling the valley with a vitality that made my heart sing.

I was filled with the spirit of springtime and an abundance of love was bursting inside me as I knocked on Matthew's door that afternoon. He opened the door and greeted me with that warm familiar smile and then reached out to hug me. He always held me tightly and I could feel his immense love as his strong arms wrapped around my petite body. He began caressing my back and my body melted into his… I didn't want to let him go… I didn't want him to let me go. Waves of rapture flowed through me… it was the most powerful love I had ever experienced. He seemed to hold me even tighter and caress me with more passion. An energy had taken us over… we had disappeared and only the love and passion deep within our souls was present.

Matthew's hand gently turned my face to look at him and we gazed into one another's eyes for what seemed forever. Then without even a thought we began kissing passionately and caressing one another… Matthews hands were so strong yet so gentle… I felt my whole body tingle with energy and wonderful sensations. Matthew began gently removing my sweater, and then unbuttoning my blouse as he began moving us out of the doorway and down the hall towards the bedroom. By the time we got to the bedroom we were both down to our underwear. Matthew looked at me and asked if I was ready and I smiled back at him and nodded gently.

It seemed like we had made love for hours, I wasn't even sure what day it was never mind what hour. Neither of us wanted to get out of bed to even eat… we didn't want to break the spell of the ecstatic afterglow we basked in.

Saturdays and Thursdays couldn't come soon enough and we would sneak away and meet every opportunity we could get in between. I remember many times when we were both out and about… Matthew would call and we would meet at a secluded park and I would jump into his car and we would make love. Matthew would especially love those times because he felt like a teenager… like he was getting away with something he shouldn't be doing.

A New Home

$\mathcal{O}$ur Saturday nights seemed to get more and more delicious, I started coming over earlier in the day so we would have more time. We enjoyed an afternoon hike up the mountain right behind his house, and relaxing in his yard that had a pond and a small waterfall. Matthew loved to dance and never needed music or any special circumstance… he loved to dance in the yard or high up on a mountain, in the kitchen, and we even danced in the bathroom. I loved it when out of the blue he would grab me and begin swinging me around… or hold me tight and slow dance with me… it was exhilarating. Sometimes he would order take out for us and often we would make meals together… he was actually a very good cook.

Everything was so perfect on Saturday except for one thing… Matthew never invited me to stay the night. I wondered sometimes why he didn't invite me to spend the night… it just seemed so much more intimate and romantic to fall asleep together and wake up snuggled up in one another's arms.

One night after a couple of weeks of passionate Saturday nights I got tired of waiting to be invited to spend the night. We had been hanging out in his bed for hours, snuggling together and enjoying very intimate close connected time and I began to get very sleepy. So I asked Matthew if he wanted me to stay and spend the night. He got a little weird and very nervous and that made me nervous. I immediately sat up in the bed covering my naked body with the blankets and began to ask questions. Matthew seemed to avert my questions and became secretive. He kept diverting from the subject and wanting to talk about something else. I kept persisting and he finally broke down and told me that he didn't live there.

My first reaction was "WHAT!" My second reaction was, " Whose house is this?" I had a whole lot of other questions too… my mind was in a very confused state. He told me that yes it was his home, but just one of his many homes. His main home was a much larger home where he lived with his wife. Again my reaction was "WHAT?"… "I thought your wife was living in a nursing home?" He said he had the mansion built as a glorified nursing home for his wife and that she has a full-time nurse that cares for her there. He said that he needed to go home before three am or else when he goes into his house all the alarms will sound off and wake up his wife. I was dump-founded and shocked. I was shocked that he didn't live in this big beautiful home… shocked that he lived in another even huger home with his wife that I thought had one foot in the grave living in a nursing home… and shocked that he must be a lot wealthier than I had ever imagined. I wondered why he needed to go home at all… wasn't he and his wife legally separated? I was tremendously emotion and left sobbing.

He called me when he got to his *real* home, and we talked but I was still in such a state of integrating all this new information it was difficult to process anything. It was still nice that he called and that he cared.

We spent the next week during our visits and phone calls working the details of the new information out. He told me how his wife lived in a whole separate wing of his home and that he wanted me to come by sometime and show me the house and the separate quarters they each dwelled in. So we made a date and I came for my first of several visits to his mansion and he toured me through the whole place. It was beautiful, ornate, vastly high ceilings, an elevator, indoor balcony, jogging track that took him from one wing of the house to the other. There were gardens, waterfalls, and patios like tropical paradises. On the ground level there was a huge multi-room area for the grandchildren with grand piano, toys, movie room, game room etc. It was quite a place, but he expressed how he preferred his cabin in the woods and his smaller home up by the mountains… they were more of an expression of who he was… this home was what his wife wanted so he had it built for her.

Money

After spending several months and falling in love with this man he seemed to be well off and generous but certainly not mansion type of mega wealthy. He often drove through McDonalds and got himself a happy meal, and he loved the 5 for 5 Arby's roast beef sandwiches. He dressed like an average guy with a flannel or cotton shirt, always with a front pocket sewed in… nothing fancy or name brand, not that I would have known anyhow. His down to earth authentic nature was one of the things I loved so much about Matthew… he was not showy or stuck up in the least.

So the next Saturday evening I came right out with the question… "So Matthew how wealthy are you?" he began to tell me he was surprised when he came for his first massage appointment that I had not known or heard of him because he is very well known in town… that he is actually quite famous and often get's stopped by strangers when he is out and about. He said that most people that grew up in town at least know of him. He also said that he is often on the news for donating money to this or that cause or helping this or that charity. I explained that I didn't have time to watch the news, some days it seemed there was barely time to eat. Matthew then stopped talking and looked at me with those handsome blue, sometimes green eyes and said, let's pour some wine first and then talk money.

We sat on his deck and watched the sunset in the west and the glow of the mountains in the east. We had another glass of wine and talked and laughed as we watched the city lights gradually light up until it was dark and the whole city glowed like a million fireflies. It was at this point Matthew seemed to have a sufficient buzz to finally answer my question. He told me that he was the wealthiest man in the state, worth several billion dollars, owned multiple corporations, and probably owned more property than 1/2 the state of Delaware. He went on for quite a while as I just listened intently. I enjoyed watching his animated facial expressions and hand gestures as he proudly described how he acquired his empire. It was a very impressive story, he had grown up very poor, gone to bed hungry many nights… he knew what it was like to struggle and to be without. He built his wealth by using his creativity, intelligence, and inspired mind… he was a creative genius. I deeply admired him, not for his wealth but for his character… he was tenacious, ingenious, practical, intelligent, determined, generous, and compassionate.

I had never looked for a wealthy man to fall in love with, my dream was always to find a loving, kind, and spiritual man… it has never mattered to me if he is rich or poor, what matters is that we are truly, deeply, and madly in love. Love not money is what I have sought so deeply ever since I was very young. I remember having debates with my grandmother at eight years old. She would tell me to find a rich man and I would tell her that I want to be in love… that I would rather live in a shack with a man I was crazy in love with than live in a mansion with a man I didn't love completely. Now I had fallen in love with a man who lived in a mansion… but with his wife… and I wasn't exactly sure what to do with all this new information.

My life motto has always been to follow my heart and all my dreams will come true. There were so many times in my life I did things that intellectually didn't make any sense but because it felt true inside my heart I did it anyway… and it always turned out magical. I knew all there was to do now was continue to follow my heart and my innermost truth from moment to moment and trust that it will all turn out perfectly. I had known for a while now that in my heart I was completely, madly, and deeply in love with Matthew. I knew in my heart that I couldn't leave him even if I tried… neither of us could deny the intimately loving and powerfully magnetic bond we shared. It didn't matter that he lived with his wife as long as they were legally separated and not intimate. We are head over heals in love… this type of love and connection is so rare, so precious, so dear. What my heart yearned for was to be with Matthew and continue our love affair and enjoy one day at a time… giving him all the love I had to give and becoming enraptured by all the love he showered upon me.

Mystery Milk Man

Everyday was a busy and eventful day as a single mom raising my children on my own. After work there was dinner to cook, laundry to wash, kids to run to sports, voice, and dance lessons… and there was dentist, doctor, and orthodontist appointments to keep, friends to taxi home, and homework to help with. One very busy yet typical day I had come home from working all day, picked up the kids, dropped my son off at baseball practice and brought my daughter to her voice lesson. While they were at their activities I stopped at the store to get some groceries. After bringing a few stray teammates home from baseball we all finally were home and it was time to make dinner. I then realized I had forgotten to pick up the milk, and we always had milk at dinner. No big deal I thought, we will just have water tonight… I will get milk tomorrow. As I was fixing our meal Matthew called to say hello.

Matthew and I had the kind of relationship where we could talk about anything… we were the very best of friends. In our conversation that evening I had mentioned off the cuff how I forgot the milk for dinner that night. It was a brief comment and then we talked about other things and soon it was time to say good-bye until bedtime. I went about the usual evening activities, picking up the house, putting in some laundry, and making sure homework was getting done, when to our surprise the doorbell rang. The kids went to the door and no one was there, but some *thing* was there… sitting on the doorstep were two gallons of milk… double bagged. I knew immediately who the mystery milkman was… my beloved Matthew. This was the first of many mystery milk deliveries. Matthew started a habit of regularly yet randomly dropping off two gallons of milk at my door… always double bagged. After that we never had a meal without milk.

Milk isn't the only thing Matthew blessed me with in all his thoughtfulness. One day I pulled a couple candies out of my purse and offered him one. We both enjoyed the caramel candy with the delicious creamy center, and I mentioned it was my favorite candy. A few days later when I came over for a visit I immediately noticed that amongst all his other treats that were set out in grand artistry on the countertop… flowers, a love note, a few hundred dollar bills, and often a trinket of some sort was a bowl full of my favorite candies.

I was very impressed and surprised that he had remembered and gone out of his way to find the candy and provide me with weeks worth of sweet treats. It amazed me because after that, almost every time I visited he had a full bowl of my favorite candies sitting out on the countertop for me. One day while I was setting up his massage table for his massage, I was looking for extra sheets and I opened a cupboard and found seven bags of my favorite candies. I could only smile as my heart filled with gratitude and love for how dear and thoughtful this beloved man is, and how fortunate I am to be loved in such a profoundly sweet way.

Matthew didn't stop at candy and milk… he did thoughtful and surprising deeds almost constantly. He found out I loved angels and soon I had more angel figurines than I had places to put them. He found out I was always looking for the best anti-wrinkle cream and he brought me a box full of very expensive creams to keep my face young and wrinkle free. After he took my Reiki course he made me a huge book on Reiki and other natural healing modalities. He bought my children bicycles, fishing poles, Easter baskets, dolls, footballs, baseball gloves, and so much more.

Matthew knew I went crazy decorating for Christmas so one day when he knew I worked late he must have been busy hanging lights all day… to my great surprise when pulled up to my home the whole house was lit up with lights. He also bought me indoor decorations, holiday music, and special holiday goodies… and he always gave me a couple thousand dollars to make sure my children's Christmas morning was both abundant and jovial. Matthew knew how close I was to my sister and so he paid for my sister and her entire family to come and spend a week in December at his cabin to go skiing, sledding, snowshoeing, and enjoying the holiday season.

One evening during my sister's visit we were all hanging out in the cabin listening to Christmas music. It was a snowy night and already very dark… we were snuggled away in the sacred and secluded mountain cabin. The adults were cleaning up from dinner and the kids were running around innocently enjoying the time with their cousins when a surprise and very unexpected visitor added some excitement to the evening. To our surprise out of nowhere a jolly old elf walked into the living room with a big red sack over his back… it was Santa Clause. No one heard the door knock or even open, he just seemed to appear out of thin air.

He visited with all the children, let them sit on his lap and gave them each a nice Christmas gift. He seemed to leave as magically as he appeared… the kids ran outside after he was gone to see if there was anyone on the roof… there was no sign of anyone anywhere but they were certain there were reindeer prints up on the roof. It sure gave us something to talk about all night and for years afterwards.

Matthew was always full of surprises, it seemed his mission in life was to do thoughtful things for us that would make a difference and bring joy into our lives. One brisk fall day I came home and my whole back yard was raked, the trees were trimmed, and some big crystal like rocks were decoratively placed along the edge of the yard… and Matthew did all the work himself.

One summer I planned a trip with my children across the United States… we had Yellowstone, Mount Rushmore, Niagara Falls, New Hampshire, Massachusetts, New York City, Washington DC, Virginia, and visits to friends in Arkansas and New Mexico planned. Even though I insisted it wasn't necessary, Matthew wanted me to have a new van so I was safe and didn't worry about breaking down. So he bought me a new van with a DVD player and navigation system for our trip around the country. It was a lifesaver and made the trip immensely more enjoyable.

Matthew loved his regular massage, and we had our regular weekly appointment every Thursday afternoon at his home. However he knew I still had a very busy massage practice with many clients, and he always wanted to enhance my life in every way. He had already helped support my practice with the new deluxe massage table… then he noticed that I would put hot rice pillows on his feet to add to his and all my clients comfort. One day to my surprise he came to my office with ten rice pillows of varying sizes and with removable covers for washing. My clients really enjoyed his contribution to their comfort, especially on the cold winter days.

Matthew was thoughtful in ways that weren't about money, like one chilly day when he lent me his jacket even though his lips were turning blue, because it was more important that I was comfortable than he. If there were only one pillow available on the airplane he would insist I use the pillow. One time we ordered the same entree at a restaurant and when our meals arrived he thought that his meal looked larger and more delicious and he insisted we switch plates so I had the better dish. He would always make sure I had the best seat with the best view, and that I was always comfortable and happy. He was a true unselfish and incredibly generous gentleman in every way imaginable.

Channeling

*M*atthew and I were having a nice visit after his weekly massage. Matthew had snacks and drinks for us to share as if he wanted me to stay for another couple hours. Unfortunately I hadn't realized he was expecting a longer visit and I had scheduled a channeling session later in the day after his massage. When I told him I needed to go, he was disappointed and wanted to know where I was going that was more important than our visit together. I told him about my friend King who had an amazing gift of connecting to and channeling information from our angels and guides. I told him that I went occasionally to get a spiritual channeling from my spirit guide. I told him the story of my first visit to this channel and our friendship and connection that ensued over the years.

A couple weeks before I had discovered this gifted individual I was sitting on my front steps with a pad of paper and decided to connect with my angels to receive information. This was a common activity that I had done since my youth, however I usually got spiritual messages of wisdom and insight, spiritual truths and understandings, not specific personal messages or names. I had never asked my guides their names and they never offered that information… it never seemed important to me. As I sat down the first thing I heard was today your spiritual guide Sylvester would like to talk to you. The name "Sylvester" came through so loud and clear that I laughed and all I could think of was the cartoon character named Sylvester the cat… I could see the black cat in my minds eye.

This was the first time my guide told me his name and I wasn't quite sure if I was hearing correctly… it was an odd name and a cat after all, so I brushed it off and focused on the message rather than the silly name.

One afternoon I came upon the local new thought newspaper with all the advertisements and articles on healing, environment, health, and well-being. I felt a strong pull to look through the advertisements…it was then that I saw the advertisement for channeling and decided to call and ask some questions. I called and King's wife Jewel answered the phone and she was a jewel of the highest kind. Her kindness and patience really impressed me as I asked my questions. I told her how I had been channeling information since my youth, and was very careful because I knew a lot of people who claimed to channel yet through experience I discovered that they were more accurately asserting their ego rather than channeling. I expressed how I was seeking spiritual guidance rather than psychic information and I wanted some insight and clarification on personal issues. Jewel was amazing in addressing all my questions and due to her nurturing and deeply loving energy I made an appointment.

King went into meditation and soon began speaking… he said he was my guide and told me that his name was Sylvester… my heart nearly dropped. I hadn't told anyone about the channeling I had received a couple weeks prior and to have that same very unusual name channeled by a complete stranger seemed way too coincidental. The channeling was profound, it seemed this guide Sylvester knew me more than I knew my own self. The channeling was totally empowering while still giving me direction and insight. My guide didn't tell me what to do, he gave enlightening information to consider and assist in making my own decisions. I was delighted not only with the channeling but with the energy, authenticity, and love of this beautiful couple.

Matthew became very interested in meeting these people and receiving his own personal channeling, so we set up and appointment. The next time we got together Matthew was beaming with joy as he held a seven page typed document. He was so excited to share his channeling with me he could hardly contain himself. He read it to me intently inserting his own reflections from time to time, and commenting on how accurate, informative, and inspiring the message was for him. When he was done he handed me my very own copy of his personal channeling, something I have kept safe as a treasure to this day.

A few weeks later we decided to go to a channeling session together. We visited with King and Jewel for a while before the channeling and it felt like we were all old and very dear friends… there was a level of comfort and ease as we all talked and laughed together. Finally it was time for the channeling and King began to enter into meditation and we all waited for the message.

Hello, this is a soul aspect of Matthew being channeled through King and Matthew wants to tell Ananda this story himself.

France is one of our most important past lives. We met when I was 13 and you were 14… it happened by accident, at least so we thought. My family was visiting in a little village in which you lived. Not far from this village was a forest. You loved the forest and on this particular day, I wasn't happy with having to visit the people who lived in your village… so, to escape, I went into the forest.

I was hypnotized by the forest… I didn't know why… on the surface it was just like any other forest… I wandered through it, searching for something but I had no idea what I was searching for. The sounds of the forest were soothing but one sound that I began to hear didn't seem like it belonged in the forest. The closer I got, the more I realized that someone was crying. I tried not to make any noise as I approached this person but I was trying to be too careful and in doing so, I fell. When my body hit the ground, I moaned and it startled you. You turned around… you stopped crying for a moment. You really couldn't see anyone because I was lying on the ground.

When I moved and tried to get up, it startled you even more and you began to run away. I yelled for you to stop but you didn't so I chased after you… I wanted to find out why you were crying. You kept running… I kept running after you begging you to stop. Finally, I couldn't run anymore and I stopped and somehow, with being out of breath I asked you to stop one more time… and to my surprise, you did. You turned around and saw me in the distance. We slowly walked toward each other, curious, a little cautious but neither one of us could stop from walking toward each other. When we got face to face, we both tried to say something but we couldn't… we just stood there and looked at each other. As we looked at each other we felt comfortable… we felt safe. We finally did find the words to say 'hello' and introduce ourselves. You had forgotten that you were crying and I had forgotten that you were crying. We were young… we didn't know what was happening but we felt that there was so much more… it almost felt that we were looking at ourselves in each other. Oh, we could see the physical differences… I was darker… you were lighter… I was taller… I was heavier… but somehow those physical things didn't exist as we were looking at one another.

We spent several hours in the forest… you showed me all your favorite spots. You knew that you were going to get in trouble for staying in the forest so long but that didn't matter to you. We finally had to leave the forest and return back to the village. We promised each other that we would meet in the forest the next day… we picked a spot… we picked a time.

The next day came and I waited at that spot… I waited all afternoon. I left when it finally started to get dark. I went back the next day and waited again but you never came. I wondered why so I went the next day to search for you. I finally found where I hoped you lived. I saw you locked in a room… you couldn't get out… you were staring toward the forest.

I waited until dark and snuck up by the room where there was a tiny window that earlier you had been staring out. I whispered your name and you came to the window… both of our lives stood still in those few moments. We had less than a minute together before we were interrupted by your father… he had heard a noise and was still angry with you. I told you that we were leaving and I promised that somehow, some way I would come back and then I ran so that your father wouldn't catch me.

After those few moments, both of our lives ended. It wasn't until a year and a half later when we finally met again that our lives began.

Spiritual Retreats

I taught several spiritual courses as well as facilitated monthly meditations and kirtans. My Reiki course was the first of many courses that Matthew attended. It was a class of eleven students and Matthew kept everyone entertained during the class… not only did he have the very best questions and jokes, he had information to share that although very enlightening at times went way off subject. Needless to say that particular class was unforgettable and finished an hour later than scheduled. It has been ten years since that class in 2002 and I still have students from time to time mention how memorable it was to have him in the course. After that first class Matthew became fascinated with a different type of healing than he had ever known.

Matthew was passionate about healing most all his life. He told me how when he was a young boy he would visit the local doctor just to talk and pick his brain. He dreamt of being a doctor all his life and he was accepted into medical school but his father wanted him to do a mission with his church, which he did and never became a doctor. Fate would have it though that he became a pharmaceutical sales person and his job had him in hospitals everyday visiting doctors. He was a fascinating man and was always observing what was going on and imagining how it could be done better. One of his motto's in life was "there's got to be a better way". With this one single motto he saw things happen in the hospitals that could be done so much better and he went on to invent many life saving medical devises that have saved hundreds of thousands of lives.

His passion for healing was great and he contributed to medical healing far beyond what he could ever comprehend as a child dreaming of being a doctor, but he still wanted to do more. So he began joining me on spiritual quests and taking spiritual healing courses with me. Our travels began as small trips but eventually they reached outward to more exotic far away places. Matthew had memories of places he had been in the past that he loved and he wanted to share those places with me.

I remember the first course we took was a weekend at a ranch way out in the desert. We walked into a rugged western style reception area with many animal remains on the walls. The husband of the women who taught the course was checking us in and he became very anxious that we pay for our course right away. Matthew walked out on the patio to view the beautiful western landscape and this man got upset with Matthew as if he was trying to sneak into the course without paying. I laughed to myself thinking how generous and responsible Matthew was… just soaking in the experience for a moment… enjoying the moment and the scenery. Matthew didn't flinch, he handed him several hundred dollar bills and smiled and said keep the change.

Later that day in our room we snuggled and Matthew wanted us to breath together… synchronizing inhales and exhales as a way to deepen our intimacy and connection. We breathed together and we looked into one another's eyes and we felt a love we had never before experienced… a connection so deep, so eternal. He was always inventing spiritual exercises for us to practice that would deepen our love and bring us closer together. It was beautiful and sweet but there were times I resisted it and felt controlled. Sometimes the connection felt so intense it became frightening. I wish today I hadn't resisted it ever… I would do anything to have the opportunity to practice those deeply loving exercises with him again.

Later that evening there was a sweat lodge ceremony and Matthew chose not to participate but I went. I missed him and I left early… as I exited the sweat lodge I immediately saw Matthew's silhouette standing there in the dark, waiting for me. He came to me and held me and said he wanted to be sure I could find my way back to our room so he waited. That was just how he was.

I remember soon after I met Matthew I had gone with my boyfriend Philip to a course in New Mexico. I would walk about two miles back to where we were staying… the weather was nice so I wanted to walk… however it would have been nice to walk together. However, both days I walked alone with no one to escort me home. At that time Matthew and I had just recently met and hadn't even been dating, but I remember thinking as I walked home alone from the course that without a doubt if I were with Matthew he would be standing there waiting to walk me home. It was just an absolute knowing, that is how he was, that was the type of man he was… as giving as any man could ever be in every way possible. Philip thought I left him because Matthew had a lot of money, but it had nothing to do with that. Phillip loved me very much, but Matthew gave his whole heart to me… he went the extra mile every time. The difference was not in money it was in the generosity of heart… Matthew had the ability to give love without measure.

One of our earlier trips was to a bed and breakfast he owned in California… he was excited to show me a venue for spiritual classes we could teach together. When we arrived in the evening they had a lovely meal ready for us. We went on a nice summer walk down the street, I remember as we held hands he began to swing our hands and then he began to swing me around and before we knew it we were dancing wildly in the middle of the dirt road and singing at the top of lungs. He was a great dancer and when he spun me around my heart panged. I felt so alive, happy, and free, I felt like a teenager. We were laughing so hard I thought I'd peed my pants.

He brought me back to our room with fancy furnishings… the room was very clean and upscale. He immediately went into the bathroom and started to fill the Jacuzzi. He invited me into the bathroom and I touched the water and it was burning hot, so he added some cold water until it was the perfect temperature. He smiled and said it is always safer to have it hotter at first because it is much easier to cool it down than warm it up. I slipped into the tub and he pulled my body close to his and began caressing me. Neither of us spoke a word as he continued to caress my shoulders and arms, then his hands moved down toward my stomach. He ever so lovingly caressed my stomach as I melted into bliss… my entire body pulsating. Soon I could feel his hand rub my inner thigh and with every stroke his hand slowly moved further up toward my vagina. Before long he was driving me crazy with passionate sensation. He moved his body even closer to mine and I could feel his hard penis pressing up against my leg. I gave in to the passion and melted into rapture as we spent the next couple hours ravishing one another in the Jacuzzi.

The next morning before I had barely woken up he was obviously in a very sexy mood. He began touching and kissing me all over waking every cell of my body up in a delightfully sensual manor. After we had been making love passionately for quite a while I had noticed a crowd of firemen gathering in the parking lot. Our blinds were partially open and they had a clear view of us making love. I told Matthew about the men outside and he quickly popped up completely naked and shut the blinds. We both cracked up in laughter, never really knowing if anyone had seen us making love or not.

We continued to enjoy some great spiritual quests…an extensive shaman training, channeling workshops, week long kirtan celebrations, Harvard Spirituality and Medicine, Dances of Universal Peace weekends, and many more. In the few years of knowing and loving Matthew he had also taken every course I taught, including a Reiki course, a year long Course in Miracles course, an intuition course, a meditation course, a living in oneness course, and an abundance course. I had taught all these courses for years, however I felt Matthew could have taught them all better than myself. I felt almost embarrassed having a multi-billionaire take my abundance course… who was I to teach a multi-billionaire about abundance?

Matthew was not a shy person, he was the type of guy who if he wanted to make a U-turn, the medium strip was not an obstacle… often in public places he would walk right up to the front of a long line of people to have his question answered. He was bold but always kind and loving. So as you can imagine, he gladly contributed his ideas and views in all the classes I taught. It wasn't long before he was an official co-facilitator teaching all my spiritual classes with me

We found that the combination of my teaching style and his contributions to be a alchemy of souls that resulted in a room full of people who were greatly impacted and transformed by our workshops and classes. We received feedback on what a great team we made and how helpful our classes were for people. We began teaching locally and quickly began teaching in other states, and even some outside the country. What I loved about Matthew was that he thought differently than I did, our brains worked differently and that provided a richer and deeper experience for everyone in the course or retreat.

Most of our memories were fun-filled endearing moments we both cherished in our hearts, but there were also some heated moments. One such heated moment was while we were driving to an annual Dances of Universal Peace three-day retreat in Lava Hot Springs, Idaho.

We drove north on a cold and snowy December morning. To this day I don't remember what Matthew said to make me so mad, but I was enraged. I demanded he pull the car over so I could get out. I just wanted to get away from him, I was so angry. He refused to pull over and I got even angrier and began opening the door while he was flying down the road at 70 miles per hour, so he pulled over and locked my door. He looked at me and said "your red hair is really on fire, and I will do anything to keep you from getting out onto this highway on a winter day with no exit in sight. You just tell me what I need to say or do to make you feel safe and ok and I will do or say it." I completely melted, started to cry and reached out to give him a big hug. I told him that he was the most wonderful man in all the world, that what he said was the perfect thing to say and I told him how very much I loved and appreciated him. We hugged and kissed for a long time and merged into a sweet and blissful union… all while still parked on the side of the busy highway.

The retreat was amazing and we met a lot of wonderful people. Matthew enjoyed the Dances of Universal peace because he loved to dance, but mostly because they honored all religions and spiritual paths as true, divine, sacred, and holy. He was very unique in how he loved… he never focused on the differences in people… he loved and honored everyone and every path. He felt no division between himself and others… he saw everyone as the same, as a brother or sister soul… as a part of himself… as part of God.

At the closing of the retreat we had two hours of kirtan chanting and Matthew fell in love with bhakti yoga. I had experienced bhakti yoga in the late 1970's while visiting ashrams and yoga retreats, but it was completely new to Matthew. He was able to arrange for the gentleman who facilitated the kirtan to facilitate kirtan celebrations at his home for our local spiritual community. This began many new adventures and experiences with our new bhakti yoga friends.

Matthew was attending a spiritual healing course I was teaching when I instructed the group to draw shaman sand paintings. I gave all the detailed instructions on how to draw a sand painting on the ground outside in nature. I was walking around the area when I heard Matthew calling me over…he was beaming with an ear-to-ear smile and his chest was all puffed up. He waved me over to come look at his sand painting, as I walked over he said to me, "I just know mine is the best." I thought for a moment to explain to him that this was not a competition but I didn't mention anything in order not to deflate his excitement. I followed him into a grove of trees and he proudly showed me his masterpiece. It certainly was not like any sand painting I had ever seen and his masterpiece had exemplified so that Matthew always lived outside the box, open to all possibilities, and unattached to anything being a certain way. I looked with amazement as he glowingly described all the aspects of his work. It was certainly not done on the ground as I instructed… it was in the v of two split off tree trunks and it was not linear but three dimensional and large… I would say a mini teepee of sorts. He had piled sticks up to make a tent-like structure and had many things inside the structure including rocks, sticks, seeds, and some coins and candies he had found in his pockets. He also decorated the outside of the tee pee with feathers, berries, pine needles and flowers. It was way out of the box… not anything like what I had instructed but I loved it and it made me smile… and he was right… his had to be the best. It reflected Matthew and the unlimited being he was and the vast imagination and inspiration that always flowed through him.

At a spiritual channeling retreat in Palm Springs California we had several personal channelings about our soul connection and the love we shared from many, many past lifetimes of being together. We were channeled a special ceremony to do together in the woods. In the instructions we were to stand about 20 yards apart from one another, then slowly walk toward each other. As we walked toward one another we were to look in the others eyes and send our love and gratitude each other. As we got close, we were to come close and then move a couple feet away, and to continue this moving closer together and further apart for several minutes. Then finally when it felt the perfect moment we were to embrace one another and hold each other for as long as we wanted. This was symbolizing the merging of our souls… two becoming one.

We found the perfect wooded area to do our ceremony. We began walking away from one another and when I turned around Matthew was gone… he was nowhere in sight. I waited a while and still no

Matthew anywhere in sight. So I began looking around for him and I couldn't find him anywhere… I was completely confused. Where had he gone? Is he ok? Is he upset? Did he not want to do this exercise? Did he get lost? Nothing seemed to make any sense, so I continued to look around for him, but not straying far from our original spot. Eventually I just gave up and I sat on a rock at our original spot and waited for him to return. I prayed to my guides and angels fervently about everything, it was a powerful time sitting there alone, praying and pouring out my heart and soul. I just continued to meditate and pray… there seemed nothing more to do.

After about a half hour of waiting I noticed something up at the top of a rocky hillside… I saw Matthew's red hair shining in the sun. He waved to me with both hands and it was too far to make out his facial expression, but I was certain he was beaming with his ear-to-ear smile. As he got closer I could see that my assumption was proven correct and he bounced into the ceremonial area wide-eyed and smiling as if nothing had happened.

He stopped about 20 yards from me and began walking very slowly toward me… I couldn't believe it, now he wants to do the ceremony! I got off the rock and began walking slowly toward him, watching his beaming face full of love and joy. I was so glad to see him and felt so much love and gratitude as I walked slowly toward him. The love and gratitude built as we moved closer to one another and soon we were a couple feet apart. We then repeatedly moved closer together and further apart like we were two waves dancing in the ocean… the love built and it was too much to contain within… it was overflowing and bursting outward. Then finally we embraced and held one another for what seemed forever, but still not long enough. It was a beautiful ceremony and I felt so embraced by his love… I felt ecstatically one with him.

Even before this ceremony whenever we held one another our energies merged in a way that was completely blissful… it was a euphoria I had never before experienced and after this ceremony our ecstatic connection amplified more than ever before. It seemed whenever we were in one another's arms that our individual selves disappeared into one pulsating, ever-expanding, and ecstatic energy field.

I asked him as we hiked back what had happened and he said, "What do you mean?" I said, "You disappeared for a long time, where did you go, what happened to you?" He said, "We were suppose to get lost a while and then find one another, and then do the ceremony." I was surprised because I never remembered hearing those instructions and when we returned to the hotel I reread the channeling instructions and didn't find anything about getting lost and finding one another. Matthew's brain just thought differently than my brain, and that was a good thing… it was how he became the creative genius and world-renowned inventor that he was. Maybe that was exactly how spirit wanted the ceremony to unfold… of course it turned out exactly as it was meant to turn out.

Matthew grew more and more passionate about New Thought theology and he became very involved in the local church I had established and directed for several years. He became an ordained Minister and a board member of the church and offered his expertise at the board meetings. He always brought the food and the entertainment to what used to be very boring board meetings.

As Matthew and I travelled out of state to co-teach courses on spiritual healing, A Course in Miracles, non-duality, and channeling our love deepened and we learned more than we ever imagined. With Matthew as a co-facilitator the classes evolved… we worked excellently as a team. He often enjoyed taking over the class, and people loved it because he was so charismatic and had a way of getting the spiritual message across with humor and lightness. Matthew was as passionate about the philosophy of oneness and non-duality as I was, and together we made a dynamic team and always had classes with more people than we had chairs to put them in.

He was amazing with people and my heart explodes with joy to think of all the people he helped become spiritually free

What was extraordinary about Matthew was that he loved all people and all religions and spiritual paths… even the non-spiritual paths. He would tell people in our classes how God excludes no one from His love, that there are many paths up to the mountain summit and God doesn't care what path you take. Matthew donated to many churches and organizations in town, he saw the divine within every organization and every person, regardless of the any conditions.

As we grew together in our teaching experiences our love also grew deeper. I couldn't imagine life without him… I couldn't image a day without him. We really enjoyed travelling because we could be together everyday.

We decided to start teaching some courses out of the US, and that began a whole new adventure.

Channeling France

Let's get back to France… you were a child who lived with your head in the clouds. Somewhere inside you, you knew there was a part of living that you hadn't discovered yet. I was the same way… you were very patient about it and I wasn't.

From the day that we separated from each other we thought of each other all the time. Your father in this time was not a mean man… the times were very different… daughters were treated differently than sons. Your dad was setting up the rest of your life at the time we met. He was trying to work a deal out where you would be wed to someone for a price. You didn't know about this when we met but you did find out about it a year into our separation and when you found out, it made you think of me a lot more.

My family wasn't poor but we weren't extremely wealthy and my father had plans for me too. He wanted me to further our family name and take a position that would help our family through several generations. I was taught how a young man was suppose to act… I was taught what to say… what not to say. When I was with you in the woods, I was myself… I didn't have to act any particular way… I didn't have to watch what I said.

When I got back home from our first meeting, my father piled many lessons on me and there was always someone making sure I was where

I was suppose to be. During all my lessons it was hard to concentrate, I thought of you all the time. The lessons had been a way of life… I was used to them but now they were a prison… they were keeping me away from you. I promised to return… it was my intent to return in a few weeks but it was many, many weeks.

During that time, you were beginning to think that I had forgotten you. What kept you going was that every time you thought of me, the emptiness inside you went away a little bit and you somehow believed that if it went away then there was a reason for us meeting. We didn't forget about each other. My lessons suffered and it was noticed… of course, there were punishments, thinking that they would actually be able to stop me from thinking about you. In some ways the punishments made me stronger… they made me think of you more. I knew that I had to leave… leave my family, leave the studies, leave the whole area. I knew I needed to find you and go somewhere else. I didn't think about how I could do all of this and what would happen after this was done… how we would live and where we would go… none of those questions entered my mind. I just knew what I had to do.

Your father was making plans on having you go live with the person you would eventually end up with. It was kind of a trial run to see if he was pleased with what you could do and if he liked what you could do, and then the deal would be done.

Two weeks before you were to move, you had been depressed all day. Even thinking about me could not raise your spirits. You had tried to talk to your father but your father didn't want to hear anything you had to say and would always stop you before you could get much out. You hated to think of what your life was going to be like. All day long you were sad… you didn't want to eat… you didn't want to move… you didn't want to work or even go into the woods.

Then, in the evening, something hit you so hard, a feeling that almost knocked you over. This feeling that came over you was to get prepared for a journey but not the one you were expecting. This feeling was so strong and powerful that it almost made you move... it had a force behind it... you were no longer depressed... you were no longer sad... you had an energy and you had many things you needed to do. Your father thought you were just taking care of the house and chores... you were cooking... you were cleaning. What he didn't realize is that every time you did something, you put a part of it away for this journey. If you were preparing meals, you hid some of the food. You hid some of your clothes... you hid blankets. You hid many things that somehow you knew you would need.

This went on for a few days... your father was thinking that he had finally gotten to you and his words had sunk in and you were excited about what he had set up for your life. After you had done all this preparing, it was evening time. You had worked all day... you finally felt satisfied that you had what you would need so you thought it would be a good time to sleep. You tried but you couldn't... your eyes were wide open and the more you tried to fall asleep, the more wide-awake you became.

The night that you got the feeling you would be taking a journey was the night that I was finally able to escape from my prison. Somehow you knew that I was on my way. All I knew is that I had to get away and an opportunity finally came.

On this particular night there was a big presentation. All the fathers were proud of their sons and their accomplishments. One by one we entered this large room, begging for approval. I was towards the end of the line and as fate would have it, one of the boys toward the front of the line tripped and fell and was cut... there was a huge delay. Everyone was either trying to help or trying to find out what had happened... I slipped away. I left everything... I had the clothes on my back and a couple of things in my pocket.

I wasn't sure how everything was going to work out but I knew this was my chance. I felt, for a minute, that the boy who had fallen, had fallen for me. I had been guarded for so long and I knew that this young man would delay things long enough for me to be a long way away because I knew that they would search the building first and in this particular building there were many places to hide. They were always searching for a missing boy… they would always find him a few hours later but for the boy, it was silence for a little while… it was being left alone for a little while.

I knew the country pretty well… I knew where to go to avoid contact with other people so no one would recognize me. No one would have any idea which direction I would go… so, by the time they would start searching away from the area, I would be a day ahead of them. For food I grabbed anything I could from the farmland along the way.

Now on the night you couldn't sleep… that is the night I reached your house. You became anxious… I kept my distance until I could have some idea of what was going on in the area. I needed to make sure that everyone was asleep. It was very, very dark but because you couldn't sleep, you had a candle going. It wasn't enough light for me to see where I was going but it didn't matter.

I finally approached where you were and you could hear things outside… you stepped to the window and saw shadows… you weren't frightened. You could see a figure approaching and then you realized that it was me. You tried to contain yourself, afraid that we'd both be discovered… you snuck out and we both felt as if we'd never been apart. We embraced but we both knew we needed to go and you realized that this was the journey you were preparing for.

You led me to the spot where you had everything hidden. I was surprised… I couldn't believe how you could know and how you could be prepared… you had no idea I was coming. We grabbed the things and quickly left. We didn't have much light because we didn't want to draw attention to ourselves… we figured we were safe on the main road… no one would be out at night.

As soon as we were far enough from your house, we stopped and held one another for as long as we felt we could. Then you asked me if I was hungry… I said yes… I hadn't eaten much all day long. You took out some bread and as we were walking, I ate the bread. This night we thought we were running away, running away from lives we didn't want but we had no idea that we weren't running away… we were actually running to something… to a life that we'd chosen.

From that night on, we loved the nighttime… the moon, the stars, the quiet, the peace, the serenity. We had no idea what was ahead of us and we didn't care… we had what we wanted … each other… anything else was just in the way. So we began another journey.

For both of us this life was very painful at times, yet, it was full of love and adventure. We became people we never thought we were. Some years later we had changed so much of who we had been that when we ran into your father, he didn't even know who you were and you wanted to keep it that way, at least for the time being.

A Family Getaway

Matthew was very sensitive to include my children in his life and our lives together. He had invited the children along on many of our trips. Our travels started off as overnights or weekend get-a-ways, and quickly moved into a two-week adventure to California. It was just the four of us, Matthew, my daughter Angel, my son Jeshua, and myself. Our plan was to go to Catalina Island, Disneyland, Sea World, and the San Diego Wild Animal Park. We came to Catalina Island first, and being an island we got there traveling across the ocean on a windy, wild, and exhilarating boat ride (photo enclosed). As soon as we landed on the island it began to pour buckets of rain and we were all completely drenched.

When we got to our hotel it wasn't quite what we had expected… the room was very small, the plumbing was old and it smelled very musty. Matthew was tired and not used to children being around, so he began to snap at the children. There was nowhere to go, it was pouring outside, there was no lobby in this old hotel, and the room was small. So I decided to fill the huge old tub in the bathroom with water and the kids and I put our bathing suits on and played in the bathtub for a couple hours while Matthew rested.

I began to wonder if Matthew's secretary booked this room for us to purposely sabotage our trip. Matthew had a secretary that my friends told me to watch out for… that she was bad news and very jealous of Matthew and I's relationship.

The next day was a beautiful sunny day and everyone was in such a great mood… it seemed the sun had moved us all into a brighter and more joyous space. We went down to the docks and Matthew booked us on a glass bottom boat tour. We were all so thrilled as we graced over the ocean watching all kinds of sea life pass by. Matthew gave the kids money to purchase food for the fish and what fun it was to see all the fish suddenly manifest in seconds. Matthew was so happy and full of enthusiasm… he seemed to be having the most fun of all.

One day in Catalina we were all walking through a neighborhood and noticed a sign saying "art open house". We walked up the hill to a very unique home that seemed to be a piece of art in and of itself… from the stone path up the hill to the diverse chimes hanging on the patio. The patio floor was all kinds of rocks and shells set into creative patterns and designs. It was the most artsy, unique home I'd ever seen. We visited with the homeowners and connected right away. They showed the kids how to mold clay, they toured us through their whole home, and afterwards we had wine and cheese and laughed and visited for what seemed hours.

When we went to Sea World Matthew knew I loved dolphins so he set up a dolphin interaction for all four of us. We all got in the water with the dolphins and pet them, kissed them, shook their hands, and we even got to go for a little swim with them. The dolphins put us on a high that just increased when we went to see the whale show. We sat up close and got soaked, but Matthew was such a great sport, he had as much fun as the kids. After the show while I went to get some food, Matthew snuck off for a little while. It wasn't until two weeks later when I received several big packages at my doorstep that I realized he had snuck off to the dolphin gift shop and bought me a dolphin jacket, watch, necklace, and a multitude of dolphin decorations. It seems his thoughtfulness and generosity never ceased to surprise and delight me.

Ups and downs

It wasn't that Matthew was perfect, and I am certainly not perfect, and we didn't always get along perfectly. Actually Matthew could make me angrier than anyone else… sometimes when I got really angry with him he would smile and look at me and tell me how cute I was when my red hair was on fire. Even when we argued however, it seemed nothing could separate us. It was difficult because there were times I wished I could leave him because of the circumstances with his wife, or because he made me so mad, but I loved him so deeply that I knew it was impossible for my heart to be without him.

Matthew was a great mirror for me… he was a great facilitator in reflecting the emotional wounds I had not healed from my own childhood. Sometimes I would recognize he was my mirror and sometimes I would just want to make him wrong. If we had a disagreement and things got intense my natural reaction was to flight and Matthew's was to fight. I remember one time he had sent me up to his house on 12st South… the house where we met for massage and our Saturday night dates. He wanted me to go ahead of him and when I arrived the whole house inside and out was full of angel decorations. Matthew knew I loved angels and as an act of love and devotion he lovingly decorated the home with a variety of different angel figurines from angel fountains to an angel napkin holder. I walked around in amazement at the beautiful display he had arranged for me. Then the doorbell rang and it was our friend King… he had come to bring something for Matthew. I told him he would be arriving soon if he wanted to wait, and so he did. When Matthew arrived he was not happy to see me sitting on the patio talking with King on his day of glory. Matthew was obviously angry and so King left right away. I had no idea this would upset Matthew so much, and his anger frightened me so I left too. Matthew being a fighter came after me, he drove to my office and I hid so he wouldn't see me. I don't think the day went anything like Matthew had expected or imagined, and I wished I hadn't left, or that I had at least not been so stubborn when he came to make up.

In retrospect I can understand how much time, thought, money, and energy Matthew had spent in making that afternoon special for me, and he was only upset. There are always things we wish we could re-do and that is most definitely one of them. Whatever the misunderstanding Matthew and I had, we always worked it out… we always got through it and returned to the love and affection that kept us so connected and in love.

Matthew and I continued to visit at his home on Saturday nights. One Saturday evening we had had an especially wonderful visit. Unfortunately though Matthew said that he needed to go home that night because he had a family event early the next morning. He said I could stay as long as I wanted and even the night if I wished. So I stayed and after he left I walked into the living room and felt such an emptiness and deep loneliness within my heart from his absence. I felt so overwhelmed with emotion I just laid down on the carpeted floor and began to sob. I don't even know how long I was crying when I felt a warm hand begin to caress me and I felt Matthew's body press into mine. He held me so tight and kissed my face. I wondered how he had known I was feeling so sad, how had he known I missed him so much… what had him come all the way back to be with me? We stayed on the floor caressing, holding, and loving one another for a long time…   I am sure when he got home that night he set off all the alarms in his mansion because it was very early in the morning.

Happy Birthday

*W*hat in the world do you get a multi-billionaire for his birthday? My children and I had gone out several times to the mall and other shops to find the perfect gifts for Matthew. I don't know if we found the perfect gifts but we had fun in the process and we were ready for an intimate celebration that would have him feel loved and honored.

The four of us celebrated his birthday at his home on 12st. I made him a nice dinner and we made a cake and we sat out on the deck that overlooked both the city and the mountain ranges. We looked out over the breathtaking view of several mountain peaks. We put on little skits and he seemed to like all his gifts. We video taped him and interviewed him asking him all kinds of personal questions about his life experiences.

At one point I asked him of all the many experiences he has had traveling the world over and meeting many famous and not so famous people, what was his very favorite experience of his entire life. He paused a few moments and we waited with great anticipation for his response… knowing he had experienced things most people never experience like flying a helicopter into an active volcano in Hawaii, discovering a patent for a life saving medical device, and cruising on a jeep with the wild animals in Africa. He had met with kings and presidents and the Dali Lama. We waited patiently and finally he smiled with joy and said to our very surprise, "This moment right now… this moment right now is the best moment of my entire life." There was simply nothing left to say, he had said it all. That one sentence said more than all the books I had ever read on being fully present in the now moment… he simply lived it and exuded it completely and absolutely.

There was a birthday gift I had for Matthew that I didn't even know I had for him, one that would bring him more joy and more sorrow than any other gift I could have imagined. We would both find out about this surprise gift very soon, and it would change a lot of things in our relationship.

Channeling France

That day we met in the woods, your father allowed you to be there. You were crying because your life didn't feel like it was your own. There were times when you tried to go against the decisions he made for you and you were punished severely for that. The things that you did where you received the knowing… like packing everything waiting for my arrival… those knowings had to be so strong for you to pay attention to them and while you were preparing, you feared your father and what he would do if he found out what you were doing.

He believed he was doing the right thing. You often disagreed with his actions but you could not voice those disagreements or you would be punished for it. So, he was telling you one thing… you were telling yourself another… however, you always had to listen to him.

In our travels when we left our families, it took us both some time to change who we were. If I asked you your opinion on something, you would not give it for a long time. You were worried that I would do the same thing. Your decisions were good decisions for you but you were never able to carry them out. Your father always stopped you before you had the opportunity. He lived in a very small world… he had many rules and those rules kept him living in his very small world. He was comfortable with what he believed… your soul screamed for more but your mind knew you had to follow his direction. You slowly learned to listen to your own ideas.

When we traveled north, it was slow at first. We tried to hide as much as possible, afraid our families would catch up to us. So, as much as we could, we traveled at night and we hid during the day.

A couple weeks into our journey, we were a couple of miles outside of a village that we had just passed… we had gotten some food there. We made up a story about whom we were and where we were going and that seemed to satisfy the couple of villagers we ran into. As we were traveling outside of this town, we kept hearing noises. The more we heard the noises, the more we worried that someone was following us who wanted to take us back to our families. We walked a little faster, as fast as we could. The noises increased as if someone were hurrying to stay up with us.

Both of us started worrying even more and finally it was clear that we could not run away… so we stopped… if someone was going to find us, then we would confront them. We stood there for a few moments but we couldn't hear anything. Whoever was following us had also stopped and as we looked back, somewhere behind us, was someone watching us. We stood there for several minutes in silence, a little frightened, not sure what to do. Finally, I spoke and told who ever it was that we knew we were being followed and the easiest thing to do would be to face us.

Now imagine the two of us… very young adults… standing there, wondering what was going to happen next and if we would be forced to go back to our families. We heard a voice coming from somewhere that said that he would not hurt us. We didn't know who it was… all he said was, "I will not hurt you." A couple of minutes passed but it seemed like hours. Finally, a figure walked around a tree about 30 feet away from us… he walked toward us. We were still worried… we did not know what to expect but we also couldn't move. We thought about running but where would we run?

The man approached us and as he was approaching, he said his name. Neither one of us recognized his name… it wasn't the name of anyone we had met in the village. He now stood right in front of us. He was old enough to be our father… a very plain man wearing a robe, trying to hide who he was. He quickly told us that he would be following us until we reached the next village. He told us that it was very important that we continue our journey until we came across a man. He gave us the name, which meant nothing to either one of us. He said that this man would be expecting us… that he knows we are coming. We looked at each other, wondering how he could know. We didn't know where we were going… we didn't know how far we'd traveled… and we didn't know which direction we were even going. We must have looked very shocked and puzzled because this gentleman continued to tell us how important it was for us to meet this man. He said he had seen us in the village and knew where we needed to go. He said he could not give us this information in front of anyone else. He gave us a big bag of food and, once again, told us he would be following us. He told us that he was there to protect us and to make sure our journey continued.

We continued to journey wondering what he meant by all of his words… wondering how someone would know we were coming… wondering when he saw us in the village. We certainly would have noticed him if we had seen him. It would take several years after that event to find out and to realize that this man did not exist in physical life. He did not come from the village.

At first we couldn't believe our eyes when we finally met the man we had been told about. He looked so much like the man we met in the dark who gave us directions. But, even with that it wasn't until much later that we realized we were experiencing something beyond our ordinary world. We met this spirit 11 different times… each time we met him he told us of someone else we would meet and would always give us a name. Yet, the few times we inquired in the villages about this person's name, no one seemed to know him and then shortly after we inquired about him, he would show up when we were alone. Each time he wore something different and he looked a little different. Sometimes the color of his eyes had changed… sometimes the color of his hair or the length of his hair was different… our eyes couldn't explain it. There was no way to explain it but he always gave us the directions to where we needed to go next. Through the course of this path, there was always someone with food and in a couple cases there was work for us to do for food and clothing.

We didn't understand what was going on yet, it was so magical… we couldn't explain who he was but we accepted him and we looked forward to seeing him. When we finally realized who he was, we realized the path we needed to follow. We realized that our lives contained a map, a map that led us to certain places and to certain people. The last time we saw with our eyes our friend and travel guide he showed us the evolution of the 11 characters he had been. We saw, with our own eyes rejecting the possibilities, we saw him change… something so physically impossible…we saw.

After he had appeared a few times we did not question whether we had made the right decision or not. We have never experienced a life so powerful… we knew we did the right thing.

For us, this life will be about making our own decisions and rediscovering the power we have. In France, our lives were led by a more powerful force than we could ever imagine but, in France, we never believed that power came from us. We believed that it was our traveler's power. In France it was our power, too, but we couldn't acknowledge that.

We set up lives to learn things, to change things, to discover things and we set up lives to love.

Betrayal

As we took off to Boston both Matthew and I glowed with love, joy and anticipation of this spiritual adventure that Matthew himself had discovered and planned. We landed in the early evening and it was brisk in Boston, almost cold, neither of us was used to the humidity. Once we settled into our room Matthew immediately began filling the Jacuzzi and pouring us a glass of wine. It was a grand idea and it seemed as soon as I had unpacked my essentials and was finished making myself at home the hot bath was ready to warm our naked bodies and cold bones.

One glass of wine led to two and that was most definitely my limit, but Matthew chose to have three. We were having a wonderful time talking and rubbing each other's muscles and enjoying being together when clear out of the blue Matthew asked me about Daniel. Daniel was one of my clients who had a crush on me, but whom I had clearly told I was unavailable and definitely not interested in a relationship. I was surprised because I had never mentioned Daniel to Matthew or anyone for that matter. I had many clients and I highly respected all of their confidentiality and never mentioned their names or circumstances to anyone. I couldn't imagine how Matthew had even known the name of one of my clients. I was in such surprise by the question that I ignored it and just looked at him probably in a somewhat startled and confused manner.

His comment began a series of emotions within me that seemed to grow throughout the retreat. But that wasn't the only thing growing inside me, Matthew and I seemed to both catch a bug that made us both sick during that trip and we found it difficult to fight the bug. We became nursemaids to one another and watched out for the other as the nausea and vomiting seemed to come and go unexpectedly. We got out only once… we walked to a nice restaurant in Boston and enjoyed the charm of the quaint city. We promised one another that when we got back home we would visit our doctors to make sure we were both in good health. However there was another thing to deal with before we arrived home, and that was the energy growing within me that something just wasn't right, that Matthew had something he was hiding from me.

After our plane landed and we found our car I insisted we not leave the airport until he told me what he was hiding. Matthew denied he was hiding anything, but I had such a strong intuition that he was hiding something I didn't back down. I told him I wasn't going to leave the airport until he told me. So he began telling me some lame story that was so lame I totally forget it. After he finished his story I told him no that isn't it, that doesn't feel right, it is something else he is hiding from me that I can feel inside that he needs to come clean with. So he engaged in another story that I knew wasn't it. I was determined and stubbornly insistent that he had something he was hiding from me and I wanted to know what it was.

Finally he broke down and told me that one time when my children's father came to my home to pick up the children for a visit he came across some child support checks I hadn't cashed and he took them and copied them and was very angry that I hadn't cashed them yet. He had a total of $120 garnished from his check each month that was sent to me to help support his two children. Not a lot… and certainly not an amount I depended on to keep the ship of raising two children afloat. I often saved the checks for bigger things the kids needed like orthodontist bills, or camp, etc. I knew there was still more to this story though… something that Matthew was holding back from me. So I demanded he give me all the information, until bit-by-bit he reluctantly shared everything… and finally I knew it was complete.

The complete story in a nutshell was that my x also found my diary and read it, and told Matthew who asked him to bring the diary to him where his secretary Glitch copied the entire diary and returned it to my home without me ever knowing. That certainly explained how he had gotten the name of my client. I had written in my journal about how stressful it was to deal with my client who had had such a crush on me. I was deeply upset finding out Matthew had read my diary… I felt violated and asked him to take me home.

We talked later that evening but I was still very hurt and my trust in Matthew had altered. I would need some time to figure this one out. Matthew called the following day and said he had gotten in to see his doctor. I was shocked at how fast he got in but he said with all the money he donated to the hospital and clinic over the years he always had immediate service. He told me that his doctor has a concern that he has cancer and that they are going to do testing tomorrow. I was surprised, but he mentioned that he had some problems in the past and they just needed to follow up. It really just seemed like a bug, I never imagined cancer… I was scared and concerned. He asked if I wanted to meet that night and I came over immediately and we talked many things out. Matthew apologized and we cried and laughed and hugged and cuddled for hours.

Renewed love

I went to my doctor just to keep my promise to Matthew. It seemed I was perfectly healthy but the doctor wanted to run some lab tests anyhow. I went to visit Matthew after my doctor appointment and we took a nice walk in the woods up at our sacred cabin. We planned a weekend getaway the coming weekend up at the cabin and were really looking forward to the time together. Matthew told me how he doesn't like me having to work so hard and needing to deal with men harassing me and hitting on me every week. He offered to pay me so I didn't have to work, to pay me whatever I needed so I could meet all my expenses but not have to work. I told him that I had clients that I had had for years… very loyal clients I wasn't willing to get rid of. I also didn't want to be dependent on him and if something happened between us then I would have to start up a long-standing practice from nothing again. So we made a compromise… he agreed to pay me four times what he usually paid me for his massage and I could keep all my female clients and all the male clients that didn't cause me problems, yet I would need to let go of all the male clients that had crushes on me or caused me any grief. I was surprised how many male clients I had to call and cancel, but there were also several I kept on… it was a win/win for us both… Matthew was very happy to do it. I was very grateful for his generosity and it certainly made my life easier and more abundant.

I was packing my clothes for our romantic weekend getaway when the phone rang and it was a call from my doctor's office. I got a bit nervous because no news from the doctor is usually good news… but a call is usually not good news. As I heard the office clerk talk I had to sit down because I felt my legs weaken from the news she was sharing. I hung up the phone and remained motionless until my children came home from school. My daughter asked if I was ok… that I looked very pale. I said that I was fine and I began to visit with them and find out how their day at school was. We had our usual Friday evening with pizza, hide and seek tickle, and a movie… but my thoughts were elsewhere and my mind quite distracted by the news from the doctor's office.

Saturday morning went by fast and soon it was time to bring the children to their fathers and meet Matthew up at our sacred mountain cabin. I wasn't sure how to break the news to Matthew, I found it challenging to get everything together, drop off the children, and get myself up to the cabin.

I was the first to arrive at the cabin, which was a good thing. It gave me time to integrate being there, I opened all the blinds and windows to air out the cabin, I filled the bird feeder with peanuts, and put on some calming music. I decided to sit out on the back porch where our two chairs sat side-by-side overlooking the stream, pond, pines, and aspens. It was relaxing and the aroma of the mountains seemed to sooth my soul.

Before long I heard the front door open and my heart seemed to pop out of my chest… I knew I would have to share the news with Matthew and I was not looking forward to it. It was only moments when he bounded out onto the porch full of enthusiasm and joy. It was his natural way to be full of life and cheerfulness… it was one of the things I loved so much about him. He immediately asked me what was wrong… he was very intuitive as well as jovial. I knew it was no use delaying the news, and it was better to get it over with than to put it off and worry about telling him, so I invited him to sit down. I told him there was something important that I needed to tell him, which concerned us both. He was fully attentive and asked me to please share. I reminded him about when we had been on the advanced Theta retreat and the instructor had told him that she kept seeing a child's face in his aura. He clearly remembered the conversation and how pleased it made him. I proceeded to tell him that the child she saw was growing inside me, that he was going to be a father… we were going to have a baby. It seemed before I could say another word he rushed over to me, picked me up, kissed my belly, and spun me around… he was overjoyed and excited. I was quite surprised by his reaction… he was a married man and I wasn't the wife… we had a forty-year age difference, and I was sure that his family, friends, and the public would not take this news favorably. He said he didn't care about any of that, he was so happy and he couldn't imagine more wonderful news.

He went into the house and came back with a bottle of wine and two wine glasses and said we must now celebrate. I reminded him that I was pregnant and he ran back into the house and brought out some juice for me. It was a lovely weekend dreaming about this new child, this baby that would bless our lives. We wondered if it was a boy or a girl, what color eyes and hair it would have, what it would do with its life and the difference it would make in the world. We seemed to have endless things to discuss about the child, and the joy it would bring to our lives. It was a memorable weekend filled with great love, joy, hopes, and dreams.

Renewed fear

As we returned to normal life the reality of having a new baby integrated for both Matthew and I, but in different ways. For me it was about starting over again, going back to diapers after so many years. My children were pre-teens and moving into independence, having a child would delay my freedom according to my previous plan. There was also the concern of Matthew's age and how many years he would be in the child's life and how that would affect the child. I thought about custody because I had gone through a very painful custody battle just a few years prior and I never wanted to go through anything like that again.

Matthew on the other hand had a different set of apprehensions and fears. He had very excitedly shared the news with his secretary Glitch and wasn't quite prepared for her response. She was enraged by the news and insisted that Matthew have me get an abortion. Matthew called me after the heated conversation and told me that Glitch was furious and she warned him that if the news got out it would be devastating for his reputation, marriage, family, and political standing. She accused me of seducing him to get me pregnant for his money, and that he needed to force me to get an abortion. Matthew's voice was trembling as he told me of the encounter and he was afraid and confused. He was certain though that we would keep the child… that he wouldn't ever let anything get in the way.

We met at his home a few days later to discuss everything, and I was surprised to see the obvious stress in Matthews face that day. We went into the bedroom and snuggled up in bed and held one another for an hour or so in silence, and then we began to talk, laugh, and cry together. There seemed no easy simple answer for all of this, but we were both sure that this baby was a miracle and we wouldn't let anything get in the way of this child being born.

It seemed Matthew had much graver concerns than I had, but he told me near the end of the evening that none of it was that big a deal. He already left his religion in his heart many years ago, politically he is the wealthiest man in town and most people only care about his money and donations, his family would have to live with it… Glitch was his biggest thorn… he said she was relentless in her rage and disapproval. He assumed she was more jealous than concerned for him. We left with a sense of peace, peace that our love was deep and strong, that our decision to keep and love this baby was certain, and the knowledge that we would be ok and be joyful again about the gift and blessing this new little being would bestow on us.

Matthew came to my prenatal appointments and he and the midwife got along famously. Our appointments were always jovial and Matthew asked all kinds of great questions that I hadn't even thought of. Matthew being the ultimate protector type was even more protective of me now that I was pregnant, and I loved it. We went to an attorney in town and drew up custody papers, he went with me shopping and we bought a bunch of baby clothes and looked at cribs and things.

Matthew really wanted to be a huge part in this child's life, he wanted to be there at the birth, and he wanted to live together with me, my children, and the baby… so he could be there to help with all the daily needs of the child.

Glitch had continued to press Matthew to find a solution to what she had perceived as a catastrophe, but Matthew ignored her rants and told her it wasn't any of her business. That didn't stop Glitch, she decided to give me an unexpected visit insisting I get an abortion, and her anger and rage were so intense I had to ask her to leave. I felt badly that Matthew had to deal with that on a daily basis, I knew it had become very stressful for him and Matthew's real estate attorney Devlin who was secretly married to Glitch began to put pressure and stress on Matthew as well.

Because Glitch and Matthew had previously had a sexual relationship, when they broke up Matthew had told Glitch that as long as she didn't marry another man she could continue working for him. Therefore when Glitch and Devlin did get married, they kept it a complete secret from Matthew. Matthew didn't know that the two people he had trusted so much had both lied to him for many, many years.

The Nightmare

I always would get to my office an hour before my first client, to light the candles, warm up the room, put fresh sheets on the table, and take some time to center myself in meditation to be in the highest most loving space I could possibly be for all the clients I would assist that day. Even the days I felt a bit sick and a little more tired than usual I still got to the office an hour early to prepare for my clients. I was the only one in the office building all day on Sundays, and I worked every Sunday. One particular Sunday I arrived early as always and was lighting some pine incense when I thought I had heard a noise, I wondered if it was Matthew because I knew my client wouldn't have come 45 minutes early. I called Matthew's name and there was no answer, so I continued setting up for my day. My door was closed but unlocked and very close to a back door that went out to a patio. I heard another noise that sounded like the back door and immediately I heard the doorknob to my office twist. Before I could react the door flew open and a man with a full-face black ski hat came into the room. I tried to run and get out of the room but he backed me into a corner and attacked me. He just kept punching my abdomen over and over and over again. I was in the office early so there was no one else in the building to hear my screams, and after what seemed forever he left as fast as he came. I never saw his face and he never spoke a word… he had only one mission. After he left I remained on the floor sobbing and shaking, I was in shock and pain. I have no idea how much time passed before my first client arrived and found me curled up on the floor. I didn't know what to do, I felt the need to be professional and not share my problems with him, but I desperately needed help. He was very kind to put a cancelation note on my door for all the remaining clients that would be coming for a massage that day. He helped me into a chair, gave me my phone, and brought me some water. He wasn't sure what the problem was and he didn't even know I was pregnant. I immediately called Matthew and my client stayed with me until Matthew arrived.

Matthew brought me to a friend of his who was a physician and a very kind and sensitive man. His doctor friend began to examine me, checked my vitals, and asked me a lot of questions… he was very thorough in his examination. Matthew didn't leave my side for a moment. I had noticed when I used the bathroom that there was some blood so the main concern for us was the baby. The doctor, Matthew, and I very anxiously listened while the doctor used an ultrasound to listen for the baby's heartbeat. It was one of the most frightening, tense moments of my entire life, as he searched and probed to find a heartbeat, but couldn't. He kept trying though, not giving up, but at some point I knew the baby had died due to the trauma and I began to sob uncontrollably on the table. Matthew held me and sobbed too, we just held one another and cried for a long time.

It seemed like a big grey cloud of grief hovered over me for weeks following this tragedy and it had caused a distancing between Matthew and I. Partly because I had no answers to who did this and it seemed to me it was someone in his life that didn't want this child born. Matthew didn't want to believe that and would get agitated when I would bring it up, so we stopped talking about it. Matthew seemed more tense and reactive and I was becoming more distant and cold, it was painful and I so wanted the warm, open, soft, and passionate connection we had always enjoyed. The love was so deep yet there seemed a wall between us that I didn't know how to break through to get that love back.

I knew how much Matthew still loved me, but things were different and it seemed so painful that they weren't the way they used to be. Matthew and I had had some conversations about breaking up but every time he begged me to keep trying, he told me how much he loved me, and I told him how much I loved him, but then it seemed things went back to that more distant and uncomfortable space we experienced after the baby died.

Matthew began radiation treatment for his cancer, and I tried to help him, suggesting I could take him to appointments or bring him food. I began researching alternative methods to radiation and healing cancer naturally. He wasn't open to any way I wanted to help or any suggestions I had to offer. He preferred Glitch to take him to appointments, not me. We met less frequently and sometimes I wondered if he really wanted to meet at all. During one visit we had a horrible argument and we both said things we wished we hadn't, we were angry, hurt and upset. It seemed the passion between us was taking a different form that what we were used to and the grief and anger of losing the child was still such a painful open wound. We broke up that day in the heat of our disagreement, but as I left my heart wanted to run to him and tell him how much I wanted it to all go back to how it used to be… but I didn't and he didn't run after me this time.

I took it that because Matthew didn't run after me that Matthew really wanted the break up, that he no longer loved me… but he also seemed deeply sad. I think both of our hearts broke in pieces because of the pain and loneliness we both experienced being apart. A day or two after the break-up I started receiving cards in the mail from Matthew. I was glad to receive them but was concerned because there was no special message, only his name. I was so used to his usual cards and love letters with pictures and messages and hugs and kisses. We still talked occasionally, and we agreed to always be friends. Days seemed so long and empty, almost torturous without Matthew.

I began dating Philip again, and although it helped to fill the loneliness, there was still an ache in my heart for Matthew. I really tried to make it work with Philip… he is a dear and close soul. Matthew found out that Philip and I began dating again and he had called very angry and upset a few times. He expressed he wanted to get back together but the wall between us was still there… things were still different… there was still so much pain. It was such a confusing time for me, I felt so torn up inside and unsure whom to love. One night when Philip had spent the night I remember at about two in the morning I thought I had heard foot steps in the house, they seemed to be getting closer to the bedroom, and then they stopped… I knew someone was there and that they were close… looking at me… I froze. Then I heard the steps move quickly away and I heard a loud bang on the kitchen wall. I knew in my heart it had been Matthew, he had come by in the middle of the night and seen Philip and I in bed together and left in a rage. He told me years later that it was him… he didn't have to tell me but he felt he needed to.

Matthew met another women and began dating her. He told me about her and said he wished it was I instead of her, but I was never very sure how sincere he was. I pretended not to care but deep inside it ate me up and it hurt to think about it.

We were apart for several months and during that time he reached out to my children's father trying to develop a closer relationship to him. In the end he was using my children's father to find out information about me, and it was a win-win relationship because Matthew would pay him for information and my ex certainly enjoyed the extra money.

The pain of being apart grew as time passed and as much as either of us tried to ignore those feelings they continued to surface. Little things brought back memories, there seemed to be reminders everywhere I looked, and it became very painful to be reminded. There was great affection for the people we were with however, after experiencing such a deep connection and intimate love everything else seemed pale in comparison. I loved Philip very much, but it just couldn't compare to the depth of love that I felt for Matthew.

One day I was sitting in the bleachers watching my son's baseball game and my ex and Matthew showed up at the game together. I couldn't believe it! I was enraged to see the two of them together as friends at my son's game… I was Matthew's friend, not my ex I got up and ran toward the bathrooms… Matthew immediately ran after me. He stopped me and I told him how upset I was that he would come to the game with my ex. Matthew said he just wanted to see me, he told me how much he missed me, how desperately he wanted to get back together, how lonely he had been since we had been apart and that he would do anything to be with me again. I felt the warmth I had felt before, I felt the love and the sincerity of his heart… I cried and he cried and we held one another. We went over to a nearby bench and talked, we decided to meet at his house and talk more, so we made a date for Saturday night.

Channeling France

After we took off to start our new lives, we were full of adventure. In the beginning we weren't afraid but as we continued our journey, for several weeks we wondered where we would end up. It seems that when we reached the point where we questioned too much, we would get one of our visits from our angel and we would keep going. We traveled a long time searching for what we knew was out there but we did question ourselves a number of times.

One time we even wondered if we'd made a mistake. We couldn't see what was in front of us. We didn't know where we would end up. At times that was scary for both of us. Time lets you forget and we started to forget what our lives were like before we left. We didn't ever stop but we did question…we did wonder. Once we finished traveling, when we finally found the place we'd end up, we knew that we had made all the right choices.

During this journey we stumbled across a place, at the time we thought by accident. It was high in the hills. We don't even know why we headed that direction but hidden in the hills and among the trees was a lake. It wasn't easy to get down to the lake. Once we saw it from up above, we had to see it up close. When we reached the edge of the lake, we were amazed at how beautiful it was. We felt so peaceful… we felt so sure of ourselves.

As we were admiring the lake, for some reason we both began to feel tired. We hadn't traveled as far as we normally had so it was unusual for us to want to sleep. We found a place that we could be close to the water… a place that was shaded from the sun and we both took a nap.

When we woke up we were amazed for several different reasons. The first one that was obvious without either one of us having to say a word was that nothing had changed around us. The wind wasn't blowing… the sun was in the same place. We knew we had been asleep but from the looks of things, we couldn't have been asleep more than a minute… it felt like hours though. As we began to talk about it, we wondered if it were possible to sleep until the same time the next day but we quickly ruled that out because we'd never done that before. We thought it would be impossible to sleep that long without waking up. We watched everything around us and everything was very quiet and very still.

Then you began to tell me of a dream you had while we were napping by the lake. You began to describe both of us standing next to each other looking over a field of green. Just barely into your description I told you that I had dreamed the same thing so I began to describe what was in my dream. I told you that as we were standing looking over this field, we looked down at our feet and noticed that the grass began to lean away from us almost lying flat on the ground inviting us to follow it. Then you jumped in and said that we began to follow it. We both continued to describe the same dream…we both dreamed the same details…everything was the same. We didn't know what the dream meant but we were amazed that we'd had the same one.

Everything around the lake seemed unreal… it felt almost as if somehow we were suspended in time. We began to walk around the lake to continue our journey. We never saw anyone else… we never saw any movement from anything else… there were no animals… the wind didn't blow. We continued walking not really knowing where we were going. After walking a little while, we looked around and realized somewhere along the line we walked away from the lake. We turned around… we couldn't see it. We weren't sure what we should do… if we should continue on and find a place to stay or go back to the lake and stay there for the night.

We both thought we should go back to the lake so we started retracing our steps. As we were retracing our steps, we began to talk about how beautiful the lake had been and we couldn't wait to get there again… it felt so powerful. We kept walking but there was no sign of the lake. After a while we wondered if we'd made a wrong turn. We spent the rest of the daylight hours trying to find the lake but we couldn't find it. The area looked familiar but there was no sign of the lake. The hills looked familiar but there was no lake.

We both found a spot to rest, to sleep but neither one of us could sleep. We both thought back to when we first saw the lake. We retraced our steps in our minds. We thought of how we walked down to the lake, how we admired it, how we had the same dream, how we slept for several hours, yet, we hadn't slept. We remembered the dream and the field of green… it was bright and it almost looked like it was a lake of green. We didn't understand it but as we both recalled the dream, we realized that the field and the lake had the same shape. When morning came, we still hadn't really slept. We had been talking and thinking all night.

We had decided to spend the day searching the area for the lake, that somewhere along the way we had turned the wrong way. We did spend not just one day searching but three days searching. We walked for miles and miles and miles and we never found the lake. We thought we found the place on the hill where we overlooked the lake but there was no lake. After all of our searching, we were both tired and disappointed. We both knew it was time to move on without saying anything to each other. We were both deep in thought, wondering how we could have made so many mistakes in the directions we chose to follow. Why couldn't we find the lake again? It wasn't a tiny lake…it couldn't have just disappeared.

The next day we came across a village and we asked someone, who had lived in this village all their lives, directions to get back to the lake. They told us there wasn't a lake around there. They said that we must be confused from traveling so long. There wasn't a lake close enough to get to if we traveled for a week. We didn't know what to believe… the lake was very real to us… we had touched the water… we had touched the trees… we had slept in the grass and we had enjoyed the sunshine. Our bodies had felt a part of the experience… there had to be a lake.

We continued our journey, reluctantly, both of us thinking about our experiences, trying to explain them… trying to understand them. The further we got away from the experiences, the more we thought that we made a mistake by not searching longer for the lake and we thought of how many mistakes we made in going back and searching for the lake. We both needed to believe that it was there somewhere so the only thing we could think of is that we made wrong choices in where to look.

Years later we had the opportunity to go back to that same area… we hadn't forgotten the lake. We hoped we'd stumble across it again but we didn't. One thing the lake taught us was to pay attention to everything around us. One thing it didn't teach us was that there are no wrong turns.

We still believed we made mistakes. Even after someone else told us that the physical lake did not exist, but that we had been involved in a very spiritual event… we still believed we made wrong choices.

In this life in France we had some incredible experiences and those experiences would have been even more incredible had we not held onto the belief that we made a mistake about the lake. Each lifetime is extremely unique in it's own ways and a big thing that we will be working together is to allow each experience and each event to be wonderful as it unfolds and not to look back at what we should have done or what we could have done.

You are going to begin to see more glimpses of France…you will see pictures in your mind of what it was like. You will see places in your mind that we visited and places that we stayed. You will see the lake once again but this time the lake will be in this physical life. What we saw and what we experienced was the future but then we couldn't even begin to explain it or to understand it. This lake will be very familiar to you and to me.

Another Saturday Night

$\mathscr{S}$aturday night came quickly… but it couldn't come soon enough. I had returned all the keys Matthew had given me to all his homes when we broke up, so it felt a bit sad and strange to go back to knocking on the door. I had remembered a Thanksgiving when we were together and Matthew was with his family and my children were with their father. I was alone, and spent the morning at the shelter feeding the homeless but had nothing to do all evening, so I spent the evening at Matthew's house and by just being in his home and feeling his energy I didn't feel alone. It was as if his love was embracing me even though he wasn't there. Now I had to knock and wait for him to let me in, it just seemed sad.

When Matthew opened the door, his smile was as big and bright as always, it was like the good old days, we embraced and neither of us wanted to let go. It was strange at first to be back in Matthew's house, so many wonderful and happy memories filled me, it took me some time to integrate being back there, but I was so happy and it only took a moment for it to feel like home again.

Matthew had dinner cooking and wine and cheese all ready. He had become fond of a cream sherry that had a very high alcoholic content so you drank only a small amount and enjoyed sipping it really slowly. He knew my grandmother also loved a similar wine so he affectionately named it a "nip of Nanny". I loved that name, and laughed when he told me. He invited me for a nip of Nanny out on the porch before it got chilly. We sipped together once again, talking and laughing as we watched the sun roll behind the horizon and the city lights begin to sparkle. We were so happy, it was like no time had passed and our hearts were even more in love, more passionate for one another. We snuggled up in the swing with a blanket and the passion just couldn't be held back, before we knew it we were on our way to the bedroom with a trail of clothing behind us. Matthew never went home that night, we ended up having our dinner meal for breakfast the next morning, and spending the whole day together the next day.

From then on our love only became stronger and deeper, and we vowed never to be separated again. Even when we needed to separate physically for a little while we never said goodbye, it just wasn't a word we ever used, it wasn't a word we could ever bear to hear.

Our love continued like we hadn't skipped a beat, we did some amazing traveling together and we also enjoyed the sweetness of deepening our love right at home… we enjoyed many days and nights together sharing simple daily rituals as well as some lavish far away adventures.

We took every opportunity possible to meet at our favorite place… our sacred cabin in the woods… we met every week and we especially enjoyed being together at the cabin for a long weekend. I had made arrangements for the children to be with their father for an upcoming long weekend with Matthew at the cabin… I packed my clothes, some music, and plenty of good wine and food. I enjoyed the scenic drive up the mountain canyon, accented with music Matthew had shared with me. I had always arrived first, and now that I had all the keys again to all his homes, I always opened the house up before Matthew arrived. I enjoyed setting the ambiance… filling the cabin with warm sensations so when Matthew arrived he was delighted and comfortable… there was nothing he had to do but take off his jacket and relax. I knew Matthew was weaker now after the radiation, and it helped him to come to a warm and welcoming space. As I pulled up the windy dirt road I notice the gate was open, someone must have arrived before me, could

Matthew already be there? As I pulled down the dirt driveway I saw Matthew's car, I was surprised to see that Matthew had arrived before me, I couldn't remember the last time he had gotten there ahead of me. I had hoped everything was ok, that nothing bad had happened.

I got out of my car and started pulling my bags out when Matthew came out to help, he was smiling and bounding with energy, and my mind was instantly relieved that nothing bad had happened, he had just arrived early. Matthew who was always jovial and enthusiastic was particularly happy that day, and I was so glad. I had brought him a Silver balloon that said "I Love You" and he was just thrilled to pieces to have that balloon.

He had the cabin all opened up with a big bunch of flowers for me, they were stunning… the whole cabin and especially Matthew's face glowed with warmth and love. We went for a short walk down to the ponds and along the creek just a little. He warmed my hands as we walked, and pulled me close into his body. We were so happy and in love. We walked along the creek to our special spot we called the "Kissing Rock"… Matthew named it this because it had become our tradition to stop at this rock and kiss. So we stopped to kiss and hug one another, and kiss some more… then we turned back. When we got back Matthew poured some nip of Nanny and we sat out on our "love swing" to enjoy a little wine before dinner. We have so many memories of snuggling up on that swing, next to "Tiny the pine tree" enjoying the beauty of the mountains, listening to the creek pass by, and smelling the sweet smells of the woods.

It gets cold quickly in the mountains once the sun sets so it wasn't long after the sun went down that we got chilly and headed indoors for dinner by the fireplace. It was our ritual to sit with our TV trays and eat dinner in front of the fire. Matthew and I never watched television… I actually cannot ever remember us watching a television show or movie together. We never ran out of things to share and talk about and we enjoyed one another's company so much that it never occurred to us to watch the television. We did however enjoy the TV trays and eating meals together in front of the fire.

After dinner Matthew told me he had a surprise for me, and he got up, turned on the CD player and played a song that was a poem he had written for me called "waves of love washing over me." It was put to music with beautiful male and female voices that echoed through the cabin. We held one another tightly as our hearts listened to the loving ballet. I felt so immersed in his all-encompassing love… so cared for and blessed. We embraced one another and were so full of love and passion we spent the rest of the evening on the floor in front of the fire basking in our love for one another. When we made love it was like there was only one of us, our energies merged… we both felt our separate selves disappear into an ecstasy that is indescribable. After making love we would often hold one another for hours vibrating with wave after wave of rapture.

It was after mid-night when Matthew looked at me and said that there was more to his surprise, and he got up off the floor walked over to his briefcase and came back to me. He asked me to sit on the couch and once I had sat down he kneeled down on one knee in front of me and held out a box and said, "Ananda my love, will you make me the happiest man in all the world and marry me?" Without hesitation I wrapped my arms around him and said, "Yes, of course, yes, yes, yes."

The rest of our romantic get-a-way in our sacred cabin was as deeply passionate and filled with love as the first magical day and night. Our love had reached a new level… we both knew with all our mind, body, and soul that we wanted to spend the rest of our lives together. There was a joy that filled us that was far greater than anything physical… we knew that nothing could threaten the love we experienced… it was eternally and infinitely a part of us.

Channeling France

To continue our journey… when we couldn't find the lake we knew we had to keep moving forward. We both felt there was a place we needed to be but we weren't sure where. After traveling some distance, we came across a river… it was a beautiful river and as we watched the water, it looked as if it were in a hurry to get somewhere and we wondered where it was heading, so we followed it. For days and weeks we followed it. Neither one of us had ever ventured far from our homes… we were familiar with just a small area. We could not believe there was so much beauty we hadn't seen before. When we finally got to the end of the river, it opened up into something we had never seen before… the ocean.

Our eyes couldn't believe what we were seeing. We couldn't imagine that much water. There was a small village nearby where we stayed. At first we thought that this would be the place, that we could spend the rest of our lives right there but as several days passed, we both began to feel restless.

One afternoon we were watching the activity around the ocean… there were a couple of boats and one in particular, caught both our eyes. It was a small boat with one person in it. They weren't going far out into the ocean… it was more like they were traveling up the coastline. We watched the boat and it got further and further away until we couldn't see it anymore. That made both of us wonder where this person was going and how much further you could go. So we began walking the best we could in the direction the boat had taken.

For a few days we walked… we never did see the boat again. When we stopped we found a little something to eat and we rested. We were up above the ocean and you noticed off in the distance a person standing on some rocks. Both of us had looked at that spot several times while we were resting and we didn't ever see anyone walk up to those rocks or see anyone standing there.

You insisted we walk over to where this person was standing on the rocks. I just wanted to rest but since you started walking over there, I didn't want you to be left alone so I went with you. We were still a distance away from this person when this person turned around almost as if he were expecting us. We got close enough to realize it was a man and he stared at us the entire time as we were approaching.

He said hello but this time we didn't notice anything unusual about the man nor did we recognize him or even think he looked familiar. After the first few seconds, we both realized that he was staring directly at you. All three of us were involved in a short conversation but he always looked at you and never looked at me. The conversation lasted only three or four minutes and the last thing he said before he said good-bye was, "He is waiting for you." Then he said good-bye and walked away.

You and I looked at each other…I was puzzled but you had an expression on your face that I could not describe. It was as if you had seen something completely unreal… something that you couldn't describe or define. You stood there looking at me, basically paralyzed. Your arms didn't move… your legs didn't move… your eyes didn't even blink. I said, "Let's go", because I wanted to follow the man to see where he was going. I started to walk away.

You still stood there as if you were still looking at me. I came back to you and took your hand and tried to get you to come with me but your body must have felt like the rock you were standing on because I couldn't get you to move. After about a half hour, your body finally relaxed and then you turned toward me. I felt a great sigh of relief to finally have you back. I tried so many things to get you to come out of it but nothing worked.

When I finally sat you down, I asked you what was wrong and you tried to explain to me that when the man said, "He is waiting," his face changed and you saw a completely different man standing before you… he showed you the man who was waiting.

You told me it was time to go, that there was a place we needed to be and that it would take us several weeks to get there. You told me you knew the direction and that we would be led. So, we stood up from the rock and started our journey once again.

In the days to come not once did you ever hesitate on which direction we should be going… every time I would look at an area and wonder if we should go around or up or down, left or right, before I could even get the question out, you would always choose a direction to go without really choosing. You wouldn't say, "Oh let's go this way instead of that way". You just walked as if you truly knew where you were going and had been there before.

Many years later we would find out that during that half hour when your physical body was paralyzed, your soul was seeing every place we needed to go. You saw the faces of people we needed to meet to help us get there and you also saw faces of those people to avoid. You followed all of those instructions without ever knowing them.

The journey to our place was wonderful. We didn't meet the man we were supposed to meet for months afterward but when we did, we began a journey that we'd never forget.

In France we weren't tied to anything… we were free to do what we wanted when we wanted. At least that's the way it felt, but there were things we avoided because we both lived under the assumption that our families would be looking for us. We had no idea the distance we had traveled… we had no idea the directions we had gone. We didn't realize that it would have been extremely difficult for our families to find us. We also didn't know that there were forces to prevent us from running into them until that time when we saw your father. It was a very simple life for us. We had few possessions… we never had a lot of money but we had each other… we had food… we had a place to live and we had our journey.

The Wedding

I know what your thinking, "isn't Matthew already married?" Yes Matthew was still married, yet legally separated, so a legal marriage was not possible, but a Pagan hand fasting ceremony was very possible, and known to be much more sacred and binding in the Pagan culture than any legal marriage… it was a true bonding of two hearts. So we decided to have a Pagan marriage and hand fasting ceremony. We would invite all the spiritual community that regularly met for group meditations, celebrations, kirtans, drum circles, and channeling.

The next Thursday when Matthew and I got together he had a long list of idea's for the wedding celebration… you would have thought that he was the woman. He was an inventor and creative genius, and believe me he could invent not only life saving medical devices but unique wedding ideas. There was one thing for sure, we would have the wedding at our sacred cabin and dance our first dance to the song Matthew wrote for me, "waves of love washing over me."

We had many people who helped arrange, plan, and organize this very sacred ceremony. Matthew wanted to keep the ceremony completely secret from his family as well as Devlin and Glitch… especially after the circumstances with the baby. He knew we could pull off a fabulous wedding ceremony without any of them knowing, but we needed to be careful.

One of my very best friends Star, who had been a Wiccan for thirty years and an ordained Minister, would have the honor of marrying us and joining our hearts in holy matrimony. Star, Matthew and I met several times to design a ceremony that would be sacred, unique, and memorable. Many other people helped in other facets… in the end it was more than just Matthew and I getting married, it was a community coming together to create a masterpiece of love and beauty.

The day finally arrived, and Mother Nature was very kind to bless us with sunshine and warm soft breezes. The hills were full of daisies… it was peak daisy season. All the birds and butterflies seemed to want to attend as well as the people.

Matthew especially loved when the daisies were in full bloom at the cabin. They were his favorite flower… he loved the yellow, oranges, and reds. These were yellow flowers, and often he would pick daisies for me on his way into the cabin and surprise me. I had remembered a time when I had arrived at the cabin early and was out in the back yard picking daisies for Matthew. I walked into the house from the back door and simultaneously Matthew walked in the front door… both of us with a big bunch of daisies to give to the other. While I was picking daisies for Matthew he was in the front picking daisies for me. So it seemed appropriate that we would get married on a day the daisies were in their prime.

People overflowed the sitting area… so we had many people sitting on the grass or standing behind or around the chairs. A large group of our friends made up the choir… this angelic choir of friends sang as Matthew and I joyfully danced toward the alter. Star eloquently and masterfully performed the sacred hand fasting ceremony that led us to reciting our own personal vows to one another. This was the hardest part and neither Matthew nor I could complete our vows without tears of joy. Star led a touching exchange of rings and finally announced us husband and wife and we kissed to seal the deal.

There was much merriment as we danced, played Pagan games and ate delicious food well into the evening. As the evening cooled down we built a large bomb fire outdoors and sat around the fire and continued to play music, laugh and dance. Eventually the party moved indoors and the celebrations continued late into the evening. Once everyone left Matthew and I were alone again, with rings on our fingers and joy in our hearts. He swept me off to the bedroom and shut the door.

Newlyweds

*T*here is something beautiful about commitment that I had never known… when you promise to be with someone until death do you part you feel secure and safe in the relationship and your heart is unbound and unguarded. The heart feels safe to pour out even more love than you knew it could possibly give, and the joy of giving so much love is beyond ecstatic. This is the kind of love and connection Matthew and I were so blessed to share in the time we had left together. Matthew was getting older and was more fatigued and tired… so we lived a simpler life, less travel and more blissful moments at home together, loving and being together.

Matthew always made it to my son's football games every Saturday morning. He would take us all out to brunch after his games… he even included the children's father. He did travel to Boston with me to help me find the transcripts of a book I began writing in the early 70's entitled "The Secrets of NI, Being Your Ecstatic Self."

While we were in Boston my sister offered to watch my children so Matthew and I could escape to Cape Cod for a few days. I remember the first day we drove along the coast stopping whenever we wished to get out and enjoy the entirety of the ocean… the smell of seaweed, the sound of the seagulls, and the feel of the sea breeze in our faces. It was a miraculous day, and we got so swept away by the sensual delights of the sea that we realized it was getting later in the day and we hadn't found a place to stay for the night yet. We inquired at several places and everywhere was full… no one had any vacancy. We kept driving along and it began to get dark, which made it harder to find the little bed and breakfasts and motels. In Cape Cod they don't have lit up signs but rather small wooden signs that are weather beaten and sometimes hard to read even in broad daylight. We drove down the narrow country road… once a cow path and saw a tiny motel nestled between ordinary homes and immediately parked and went in. To our great luck there was one room left… we took it. I decided I wanted to go for a quick night swim, so the lady that ran the small motel directed me down some neighborhood streets to a small beach about a half mile from the motel.

Matthew wanted to rest, so I told him I wouldn't be long. I enjoyed the summer night walking to the beach, and was even more thrilled as I slowly immersed my body in the warm, salty waters of Nantucket Sound. The wind blew in my wet face as the buoyancy of the water and waves bounced my body around, I looked up at the shiny almost full moon… all my senses where fulfilled. After a short swim I got out of the water and dried myself off and began walking back to the motel. A few moments into my walk, I saw a very familiar silhouette walking toward me… it was Matthew coming to rescue me and keep me safe. It reminded me of the time he met me at the sweat lodge several years prior… he was the ultimate protector.

The next morning during breakfast Matthew told me that although he had grown up in California, he had never actually swam in the ocean. So I told him I would swim with him in the ocean, and show him what he had been missing. I went to a local store and purchased a lawn chair for him to sit in on the beach in case he got fatigued. The day was still young as we headed to the beach with sunscreen, towels, beach chair, and picnic. It was a quiet and very private beach… we had the whole beach to ourselves. I held Matthew's hand as we slowly entered the water. We didn't need to go in far or deep to enjoy the buoyancy and delight of the cool water so we stayed a little above waist high. When the gentle waves came in they never went over our heads. It was simply exhilarating for both of us, mostly for Matthew who never had enjoyed the experience of being bounced up and down by the friendly waves of the sea. We spent the day at the beach, in and out of the water, and curling up together on the shore as we let the sound of the gently crashing waves lull us to sleep.

That evening we danced in our room to music Matthew had brought along. It was always so exhilarating being with Matthew, but dancing together was especially fun and we did it often. He would twirl me and spin me around and when I'd least expect it pull me close into his body and hold me passionately. When we would spin and twirl his eyes would twinkle and my heart would pang, and when he held me close my whole body would tingle.

It reminded me of when Matthew and I had gone to a kirtan event at an ashram in Massachusetts. The first night of the event at about half way through singing devotional chants I got up to dance and Matthew joined me. We danced and twirled in ecstatic joy together the rest of the evening. When the event was over several people came up to us and told us our energies were so magnificent to watch, that our combined energy field was expanded and absolutely beautiful when we were together. Everyone thought we were married, and that was before we had our marriage ceremony.

The next morning of our Cape Cod adventure we decided to wake up early and watch the sunrise over the ocean. Matthew had only experienced sunsets off the coast of California but never did get to see the sun rise over the ocean… so we thought we would cease the opportunity. We woke up early and brought blankets to the beach and snuggled up together against a sandy dune as we watched the sun rise up over the ocean and turn the sky a mired of orange, red and yellow… it was a memorable and deeply romantic moment.

Channeling France

$\mathcal{D}$uring our journey to get where we were going, we came across a small village. It was unlike any place we'd seen. It was in the middle of a forest and most people didn't know it existed because for most there was no reason for them to travel through this area. There were only five or six cottages and then there was one farther away from the rest. For us, we were unsure of where we were going but you seemed to know the way without really knowing it. The village was quiet… it was in a clearing and it seemed guarded by the trees… protected by nature.

When we stepped out of the forest into the clearing, a gentleman came out of the cottage close to us. He quickly walked up to us almost as if he were expecting us but he didn't say that. He welcomed us… he was friendlier than anyone else we'd met. He wanted us to meet everyone in the village and as we approached the cluster of cottages, people came out to greet us. For both of us this was a little puzzling. How did they know we were there? We didn't make any loud noises… there was no sound to alert anyone we were there. We weren't talking loudly but everyone seemed to know. Everyone was friendly and they wanted to know what brought us to their village… we really couldn't answer them because we didn't understand how we got there.

They gave us food and asked us to stay for as long as we wanted to stay. They told us about their lives… they told us about building their cottages away from everyone else. They wanted to be free and make their own choices and live their own lives away from everything else.

During all of this time, we didn't see anyone come out of the cottage that was away from all the others. No one mentioned anything about the people who lived there… no one said a word.

They wanted us to stay at least one night so that the next day they could take us to a spot in the forest where they all would go on occasion to thank God for what they had. We agreed. We had been traveling several days in a row, only stopping to sleep so we both wanted rest. They fed us well and they fixed us a place to sleep in one of the cottages. The small family that lived in this cottage went and stayed in one of the other cottages so we could be by ourselves.

I tried to ask someone about the cottage that was away from all of the others but the more I tried, the more I couldn't speak. My brain was trying to ask the question but no words would come out. If that happened to me now, I would know that it wasn't the right time to ask, but then I was just frustrated.

We woke up the next morning to the laughter of a couple of small children. They weren't used to seeing strangers. We got up and had a big meal… the village people told us that we needed our strength for the journey to this special place… it would take us most of the day to get there and back. We followed them, not knowing what we were getting into but both feeling very comfortable and very safe with these people.

The journey was beautiful. When we arrived at their special place, they stopped and needed to tell us what this place was all about before we entered. They told us that when they were searching for a place to settle and start new lives they came across this spot. They told us that this spot led them to their home in the village.

They told us before we entered their special place, that we would see a woman in this place… then they let us in. Now, you and I were both expecting a woman of flesh and blood, a body, someone we could talk to. What we found when we walked into this place was a huge rock formation that looked very much like a woman. The formation was mostly of her head. It was amazing that the rocks could look that way… there was no evidence all around it that anyone had carved it. To the side of her there were smaller rocks that looked as if they formed an arrow pointing in the direction of where these people built their village. To these people, this rock formation was a sign from God and it was also a sign for them to believe in something more.

As we stood there, we found the formation fascinating but we didn't get the full impact of it until the next morning when we were back at the village and the gentleman, who was the first one to greet us, wanted us to meet someone else. He took us and led us to the cottage that stood by itself. Our curiosity about this cabin had grown, especially when no one had mentioned it or even acknowledged that it was there until we were walking toward it. When we were about halfway between the cluster of cottages and this lone cottage the gentleman stopped and told us that we needed to finish the journey ourselves. He said that she was waiting for us and he said that there were things that she probably needed to tell us. He smiled and walked back to the village.

He continued on and just before I had a chance to knock on the door, the door opened and standing there was a woman. As soon as we saw her face, we both realized that the woman had the same face as the rock formation in the special place. We stared at her wondering how that could happen. She invited us in. We sat down and she began to tell us the story that the villagers had already told us about them coming across that special place, but, what she added was that along the journey that these people had made several years back, she lost her husband… he died along the way. When they reached the clearing months later, she said that she saw him there welcoming her. She said that it was him who led her to the rock and that this was her place to be. He told her that she knew things and that she needed to help anyone who found the village.

After she finished her little story, she reached over and took your hands… she stared at your hands. She was silent as she was staring and we kept looking at each other wondering what was going on. We wondered if she would say something but she didn't. Then finally she began to talk… she was still staring at your hands and she said, "Your hands have eyes. They can see beyond this world." Then she let go of your hands… she got up and walked over to the door… opened the door and motioned for us to leave. There was no explanation, no further words. When we left she had a smile on her face so we knew she wasn't angry at something we had done or not done.

We both left with the strangest feeling and you put your hands up to your face to look at them, wondering what she had seen, wondering what she meant. We didn't say anything to each other until we got back to the cottage where we were sleeping. We both wondered if we should leave… things just felt strange. What we decided to do was at least wait a couple days because the next day we wanted to go back to the rock and look at it more closely.

Early the next morning we got up to start our journey toward the rock. As we made our journey there, we kept turning around seeing if anyone was following us… we just weren't quite sure what to make of this village and everything that was going on. We weren't afraid… everything just felt strange. When we got to the special place where the rock was, the women from the single cottage was already there. That was a surprise to us. She asked you to touch the rock so you put your hands on the rock, touching it in many different places. She asked you to close your eyes and to see with your hands. You did that and then a few minutes later you turned to her and said that everyone in the village believes that her husband carved the formation from the time he died until they reached the clearing and she said to you that your hands have eyes and then she left.

We stayed there at the formation, as long as we could and still make it back to the village before dark. When we got back to the village I wanted to find out what the people believed about how the formation got there. I talked to several different people and they repeated the same story you had said to the woman. I told you what the villagers had told me and you were even more confused. You didn't know why you said those words to the woman… you weren't sure of anything anymore. We stayed in this village for a couple more weeks. We didn't see the woman very much at all but the couple times we did, she always said that your hands have eyes. Neither one of us knew what that truly meant… we didn't understand the impact of what she had to say but she was right and it still applies today… your hands do have eyes.

Squirrel

Matthew's favorite place in all the world was our sacred cabin in the woods… so every chance we got we met up at TL and enjoyed the forest, ponds, streams, wild life, and especially one another's company. Matthew, like the first day we had arrived at the sacred cabin enjoyed feeding the creatures of the forest with peanuts. He would fill the bird feeder with peanuts and put peanuts on the deck railing and we would sit on the deck and watch as the squirrels and the blue jays raced to get the peanuts. Sometimes the squirrels would chase one another back and forth as they competed for the juicy peanut delights. Sometimes even the squirrels and the blue jays would have little spats. As we sat on the deck hand in hand we would enjoy these lively shows, and all amongst a back drop of mountains, pines, aspens, a babbling brook and serene ponds.

Matthew and I spent countless days and hours sitting on the back deck of TL enjoying the entertainment of the squirrels and blue jays, the aspen leaves glittering in the wind, occasional moose, and hummingbird visits. We also enjoyed the deck at night… often after a meal by the fire, Matthew would grab my hand and bring me out onto the deck and we would dance under the stars. It was one of our things, and one I will always cherish. Matthew believed there was no better view in the entire universe than the view from the back deck of TL… and I suppose he is right.

When we spent time at the sacred cabin we also spent many, many hours in bed… making love, talking, listening to music, scratching each others back, laughing, sleeping, and just enjoying the feeling of being snuggled up against one another's body. However, it wasn't always just the two of us in bed at the cabin… we sometimes had invited guests to join us in bed. It all began as we watched squirrel and the blue jays do their little dances at the bird feeder that sat right outside the bedroom window. We would fill the birdfeeder with peanuts and within minutes we had full on entertainment.

It was Matthew's idea one day to put a peanut on the outside window ledge and see if the squirrel would come that close. Of course he did, but Matthew and his creative mind, couldn't stop the game just yet. So Matthew opened the window and put a peanut on the inside of the windowsill… and within moments our squirrel friend came into the room through the open window and grabbed the peanut on the windowsill. Before long Matthew had the squirrel really working for his keep… he had a plank of wood from the windowsill to another plank of wood that went across to the nightstand by our bed. Matthew placed several peanuts along the planks of wood to lure the squirrel to the nightstand. Before long Matthew had a grand obstacle course for the squirrel having him finally end up snatching the last peanut on the shelf in the headboard of the bed. We would snuggle up together in bed and watch him come right up to our faces to snatch the peanuts. We would play this game with the squirrel sometimes for hours.

When we were sitting together on the deck there were two squirrels, they mostly took turns grabbing a peanut, but they also had their little scrimmages, which were always fun to watch. We decided they were our pet squirrels and we named them short tail and long tail… due to the lengths of their tails. It wasn't long before Matthew had both squirrels taking peanuts off the tops of his shoes, out of his hands, and even out of his shirt pockets.

Channeling France

After we left the village we continued on our way and you were less sure of where we needed to go… however somehow we both trusted that our journey was taking us somewhere. While you and I were traveling we were experiencing such great connections with each other, with nature. It felt like everything was right.

However as we were traveling we came upon an area where we both felt a little scared…we felt that it was an area to avoid. We started going around it and we felt better, but we also hurried faster. We were being watched, although we didn't know it.

Everything happened so quickly and before either of us had time to figure out what was going on we were surrounded by a group of men and they took me in one direction and you in the opposite direction. I could hear you screaming my name for a minute or so then you stopped. They took us away from each other.

We had never experienced anything like this since we had left our homes. All of our experiences up to this point had been very pleasant, even though we couldn't explain most of them. We were both frightened but most of all we both felt so disconnected from each other. They knocked me out but still kept traveling in the opposite direction they were taking you.

Your thoughts were of me and what was happening to me... you wondered where they were taking me, ignoring where they were taking you... every time you tried to speak, they would hold a hand over your mouth... they kept traveling and we got further and further apart.

When I finally woke up, I was in a place with several other men who they had kidnapped... we were really more boys than men. Their intentions were to use us as slaves for their own use. They were building something and they wanted us to do it.

You were taken to a very different spot near water. There was a ship waiting to take you somewhere else. You were to leave the next day on a journey that would take you even further away from me. But, as you were being brought to the place where you would spend the night, a young man saw you... he could not take his eyes off you. He followed where they were taking you... he stayed hidden... he didn't want to draw attention to himself. He watched you. When night came, he was still there hiding and watching. He would be in trouble himself because he was expected somewhere else and he knew that someone would come after him, but he felt he couldn't leave. He overheard two of the men talking about what would happen to you.

He waited and waited, not sure what he was waiting for but in the middle of the night... while everyone was sleeping including you... he snuck in and asked you to follow him. You were frightened... you didn't know if he could be trusted but you felt that staying where you were would cause you more pain than going with this young man. So, you followed him. You had no idea how he was able to get you away from those men and you knew there wasn't time to ask. You followed him for miles and miles.

When daylight came, you finally were able to look and see the young man and feel safe from those men. In the daylight you noticed that the young man couldn't have been more than 13 or 14 years old. He didn't want to tell you his age... he didn't want you to know. He loved staring at you… watching you… memorizing your every move. You rested for a short time and he asked you where you wanted him to take you… he told you his name was Atkinson. This puzzled you… why would this boy risk his own life to save yours and now escort you anywhere you wanted to go? You explained to him what had happened… you explained that we were separated and you explained to him that more than anything you wanted to find me.

When you told him about me, he was overcome with sadness. He tried to not show it, but he said he would help you find me. He asked you to describe everything that you could remember about the event when we were separated… what did the trees look like… what did the ground look like? To you, the ground looked like the ground, but to him, different areas had different ground. He asked you about the leaves on the trees… he asked about the sky and the position of the sun. Some things you remembered and some things you didn't. Atkinson was searching for clues… you were searching for me. You both began to walk… there were a couple of times when you wondered if Atkinson was leading you somewhere completely different and just pretending to help you.

That night, while you were sleeping trying to get your rest for the continued journey, a sound woke you up and you saw the young man watching you. At first, you were a little frightened by his behavior but then, he touched you and told you everything was going to be all right and to go back to sleep… when he touched you, you felt safe but you didn't want to go back to sleep. You sat up and the two of you talked until the sun came up. He told you about his life, which for him didn't take very long. He told you he had dreams of seeing other places, of wondering what was beyond the water that he was used to seeing. He told you that he had settled into staying and growing up in the town where he saw you and just dreaming of other places. But, he told you that when he saw you, he believed that he could find those other places. As he watched you that first night, he got caught up in a new adventure away from the limited world he had known, away from working, away from being required to follow many rules. He told you that he loved you from the first moment he saw you. He also told you that somewhere in those fantasies that night he wished that the two of you could run off together. He asked you about me and as you began to talk about how we'd met, you could see in his eyes that he was wishing it had been him instead of me.

No matter what was said and no matter what he felt, he was still determined to help you find me. He never found me though, but he tried for almost six months.

A Change of Season

Matthew and I had planned to meet up at the cabin on a beautiful fall Thursday… we always spent the whole day Thursday together at TL. When I arrived at the cabin I opened everything up and did the usual things to make sure everything was nice when Matthew arrived. I usually arrived to the cabin about a half hour or so before Matthew, but a whole hour had gone by and he still wasn't there. I walked around the property a bit and cleaned some things up in the house to keep busy while I waited and he still hadn't arrived. There was no cell service in this area in the mountains so I wasn't sure what to do. It was alarming because Matthew was extremely responsible and consistent… it was totally out of the norm for him to just not arrive after such a long time.

Once two hours had passed I just began to sob, something inside me knew something was wrong. After a good cry I got into my car and drove down to the closest gas station and used a pay phone to call him. He answered and I felt a thousand pound weight lift off my heart. He said he was sick and he was at his house at 12st South and for me to meet him there. I hurried back to the cabin to lock things up and raced to town. When I got there Matthew was in bed, he said he was on his way up to the cabin and he had to use the bathroom and couldn't be away from the toilet more than a few minutes. It was his bladder that was tormenting him not his bowels.

I had remembered having a few urinary track infections and how painful and uncomfortable it was, so I totally understood. I told him I was going to run down to the store and get some over the counter medicine that had really helped me in the past. I was very quick and offered him several options and he was very grateful.

We snuggled up together in the bed and Matthew would rest a bit and a few minutes later he would get up and run to the bathroom… when he came out of the bathroom he would have a huge smile on his face and snuggle back into bed. This went on for a couple hours… sometimes he only made it three or four minutes between bathroom runs. I kept offering to take him to the insta-care but he refused. I knew he had to be utterly miserable, I knew when I had bladder issues I was not smiling, but he continued to smile from ear to ear even in such pain and discomfort. I always loved Matthew's smile, but today I loved it more than ever because he showed me how you can smile in good times and in challenging times… you don't always have a choice about your circumstances, however you always have a choice how to react.

In our nightly call Matthew told me that later that night he did go to the insta-care and he had felt better. What I didn't know was that Matthew didn't have a urinary track infection, but his bladder was shutting down due to the cancer.

Even though I had known his health was deteriorating the news had come like a knife through my heart. I had no idea how sick Matthew was, he always seemed so optimistic and he never complained. He had hid his suffering well. I knew now that our time together was limited. I didn't know how much time we would have together, but I did know that we would make the very best of every moment we were blessed to share.

Matthew called one day and told me he was at the local hospital, and that I could come up to visit him after all his family had left. I raced to the hospital only to wait three hours before he called and told me the coast was clear. I was happy to see him but concerned for his health. He reassured me that he was getting out the next day and not to worry… that we would slow dance on the porch tomorrow.

I sat and visited with him for a few hours, and without any notice his son dropped by to visit him. It was an awkward moment because none of his family had met me or even knew about me. Matthew just told his son I was a friend and I quickly left without giving Matthew the usual hugs and kisses.

Matthew was in the hospital longer than either of us expected, but soon he was home and we did have that slow dance on the deck. We cherished every moment we had together, and the time seemed more and more precious. We still never said goodbye and we never talked about death, we simply enjoyed what life we had together as fully and deeply as we possibly could.

We had a fun tradition every time Matthew left the cabin, he would drive off down the dirt road and I would stand in the driveway dancing and waving. He would wave his hand out the window until he was out of sight. I remember the last day we spent up at the cabin, it was a glorious day, but things had changed. The first thing we both noticed was it seemed our pet squirrel was a different squirrel. Long tail was the one who always visited us in our bedroom and this new squirrel was neither long tail nor short tail. We both noticed it yet neither of us wanted to admit it… it seemed like it had an interpretation neither of us wanted to face.

We were quieter than usual that day, there was sweetness to the day but there was also sadness. It was late fall and the leaves had already changed and fell, the ant farm by the pond that we always visited had been disturbed and there was no longer any evidence of our friendly ant colony. We walked over to the stream where the tree Matthew had planted years ago stood. I had made a rock garden with flowers and a bench by his tree, and we sat there awhile, as if he was saying goodbye to the property he had felt so connected to and loved for so many years.

He drove off down the dirt driveway waving his hand up and down until his car disappeared, as he had done for me hundreds of times over the past seven years. I fell to the ground and sobbed… somehow I knew that this would be the last time Matthew spent at his sacred cabin paradise.

The cabin was too far a drive for Matthew now, even if I drove, he wanted to be close to town… close to home. It became more and more obvious that Matthew was getting weaker… the color in his face was paler and he mostly wanted to snuggle in bed and rest when we spent time together. I was just grateful to be with him, to hold him, feather his back, caress his body, kiss him and hug him. Every moment we spent together was about loving one another as deeply, profoundly, and lovingly as we possibly could.

I hadn't spent too much time at his mansion because his wife lived there, and she still didn't know about me. But there were a handful of times when his wife would go out of town and he would invite me to spend the night at his mansion. During this time that he was weaker he wanted me to spend the night with him at his mansion every possible opportunity because it meant he didn't have to drive across town to see me. So whenever his wife was not home he invited me over. At this time he had a urine bag because his bladder had completely collapsed, but he made the best of it. I remember him walking around his big mansion, taking me downstairs to get some juice, and being happy and jovial. I worried though because I knew that his children would be around to check in on him, so during the night I didn't get a wink of sleep. I kept imagining one of his children coming to check on him and me trying to hide under the covers as close to his body as possible so that they didn't notice I was there.

The very first Valentines day we shared I had given Matthew a stuffed dog, and I was happy to see he still had it after all these years… in the most honored spot in his room… on his bed… he was as sentimental as I was. The next day he wanted me to stay and visit, so I did, but I was tense knowing one of his children may come by unannounced at any time.

We were sitting in his room snuggled up on the couch and I couldn't relax, I kept jumping up to look out the window to see if there was a car in the driveway. Then I'd go back to snuggling Matthew and relax for a few minutes. I went back to the couch and began feathering Matthew's back when I heard a noise and I jumped up, grabbed my purse and as I ran toward the door… but at the same time the door began to open. I stopped abruptly when a women stood in front of me… we were face to face and it was obvious I was running out… it was awkward and I wished I hadn't tried to run off but instead just sat there next to Matthew as to not look so suspicious. Matthew had a look of panic in his face… then he saw that it was his daughter, not his wife, and he looked relieved. He told her I was a social worker that had come to visit him, but I knew she didn't buy it.

We still talked several times a day on the telephone even on the days we got together… we always stayed very connected. Then one day he didn't answer his phone, and he didn't call. I knew something was wrong… it was totally out of the norm for Matthew not to call or answer my calls. There were times he was in important meetings and he stepped out to get my call… Matthew was always there for me. As the day progressed I got more and more panicked. That night I couldn't sleep and at about two am I drove my car to the hospital emergency room. I knew I couldn't go in so I just sat in my car in the parking lot… I didn't know if he was there… there were several hospitals in the area… but I felt he was in the hospital, this hospital. I was tormented inside not knowing how he was or what was going on. I decided to call the emergency room and ask how he was doing pretending that I knew he was there. I was taking a chance because I didn't know if he was there, he could have been at home with family or in another hospital but I had to call to find out for sure.

"Hello, I was wondering if someone could let me know how Matthew Searson is doing?" "He is doing much better, he will be discharged shortly." All my anxiety and fear lifted… he was alive and he was going home.

I must have left 30 plus messages that previous day trying to get in touch with him… I later thought that he won't have the energy to listen to them all, but at least he'll know I was thinking of him. Early the next morning Matthew called me and told me he was ok. I was so grateful to hear from him, maybe now I could get some sleep.

Things were getting pretty bad, and he told me his family was not wanting him to drive to work, or leaving the house at all… but everyone knew Matthew had a mind of his own and as long as he could do it, he would. They were hovering more closely and after his visit at the hospital there was a nurse that was staying at his home during the evening and nights. Matthew had given an enormous amount of donation money to the local hospital and they were providing the best care for him, now at home.

Matthew was the eternal protector/provider and he had decided I needed a new car, even though he had bought me a new minivan just a few years prior. He wanted me to have a Toyota Highlander, and his mind was set. He was too weak to come to the dealership with me so he had Devlin go and purchase the car for me. It was his Christmas gift and his last big gift to me.

Matthew and I usually saw one another three or four times a week, and talked several times a day, but it had now been a whole week and we hadn't seen one another face to face. We had made a couple plans but he had cancelled because he wasn't feeling well enough to leave home.

I remember the very last day we were together in person. Somehow I knew it would be the last time. The kids and I had made an overnight holiday visit to my brother's several hours away. I woke up at 5 am to get home with plenty of time to meet Matthew at his home at 12ˢᵗ South. On the way home from my brother's I ran into a big snowstorm and was stuck in slow moving, sometimes stopped traffic. I was a nervous wreck and I called Matthew just to hear his voice, I didn't tell him I was in a snowstorm and worried about seeing him that day, I told him how much I loved and appreciated him. I tried not to let my nervousness come through in my voice.

Matthew wanted to see me very much, and he also wanted to see the new car he had bought for me… he hadn't even seen it yet. The traffic and the storm just didn't let up, I was at a crawl and I knew that I still needed to bring the kids home, wash the car, and run across town to his house.

I never remember feeling so panicky in all my life… it was like life or death, there was a part of me that knew this would be the last time I would see Matthew in person and I was very afraid and emotional.

We had finally gotten through the storm and were travelling at a good speed again. I was able to get to Matthew's house on time and with the car washed… it seemed a miracle. To my surprise Matthew was already there and in bed resting. I took off my clothes and snuggled into bed with him. He smiled and was so glad to see me. We spent several hours snuggling and talking… it was a precious time, yet there was a sadness in my heart knowing our time was very limited and it was very possibly the last time I would be able to snuggle up to his body, smell him, look into his eyes and hold him in my arms. I kept my composure and held back my tears as not to upset him, and I never mentioned that I thought it might be our last time together. It seemed, however that he knew as well that it would be our last opportunity to share life and love in person in these two physical bodies.

He was able to see the car he so generously gifted to me, and he was happy to see how much I loved it. It was a lovely last visit, and I will always cherish it. I cherish all the times we had to share life and to love one another with such tenderness, passion, and depth. I cherish the time we sat in the hammock under the pine trees at TL and watched birds and butterflies dance above us. I cherish the time we danced with the Shaman in Peru. I cherish the time he brought my mom out and scattered twenty-dollar bills all over the floor for her to find. I cherish the time he came to the park to rescue me when I ran out of gas. I cherish the time my chest had broken out in a rash and for days he would gently feather my chest to help it feel better. I cherish the room off my garage he finished for me so I had a space for courses, meditations, and healing sessions. I cherish how kind he was to my children, always at their birthday parties and events. I cherish how he loved me, how faithful, devoted, and true his love was for me. I cherish how safe and secure I felt to be with him, that just knowing he was there I felt like nothing could ever hurt or threaten me. I cherish how I felt when his arms embraced me… I was in heaven… no words can express the peace and happiness. I was a different person because of Matthew… he had given me a whole new view to life, he had given me courage to live a much bigger life and make a difference with my life.

A week had gone by since that last visit and I had talked to Matthew everyday, however we had been physically separated. It was painful to not be able to sit by his bedside and hold his hand and look into his eyes and love and reassure him. I was forbidden to go to the house and the separation was killing me. I wanted to be there by his side so badly I couldn't stand it. I was so tormented by the separation that one day I couldn't take it any more and I drove over to his mansion and thought I would beg his family to let me see him. I parked in the extra driveway that he had me park in when I visited him at his mansion. I remained in the car a few moments to gain my courage and think through what I would say. That is when my phone rang and it was Devlin and he told me that I needed to leave the property immediately or they would have the police escort me out… so I left.

During one of our phone calls Matthew had told me that Glitch would be taking him to the clinic the next day. We both saw it as an opportunity for us to be together in person so we made a plan. I got to the medical center an hour early as to not miss him, and I walked into the full waiting room and looked for a seat, as I circled the room I noticed his two daughters sitting in the waiting room, so I continued my way through the waiting room out the door and back to my car. I called him and he answered, he was in the doctor's office, he made it quick and told me that plans had changed and his family would bring him to appointments from now on. I told him I would wait in the parking lot so that at least I could see him as he got into the car. I stayed in my car all day until I saw him leave the center with his daughters. It was so worth the wait just to see him walk across the parking lot, see the sun glimmer in his red hair, I was grateful to be that close to him.

The next time he went to the center I again told him I would just sit in the parking lot, that I just wanted to see him. I parked in a very strategic spot that was a little distance from the front doors as to not be recognized, but elevated a bit so it had a great view. It seemed moments after I had arrived Devlin had pulled up next to my car. He told me that I needed to leave, that I couldn't go into the building and that I needed to stay away from Matthew. I had no idea how Devlin had known I was there, but I told him that I wasn't planning on going into the building but I had every right to be parked at that public parking lot. He pulled into a space near me and never left until I eventually left. But I was so glad that I stayed because an hour later Matthew arrived to the medical center and he walked across the parking lot and sat on a bench out in front. I knew he did that for me, so that I could see him and he could see me. A family member sat next to him but they had no idea I was there or that he was sitting on the bench modeling his handsome face for me. It was a precious gift and the memory of him smiling as he sat on the bench with the sun dancing in his red hair will live in my heart forever.

Matthew was now home and not going to leave his bed again, the medical center had come to him full-time now. He had many people around him and didn't answer his phone if I called. People all over town began visiting him and saying good bye, there were lines of people, and police were parked at the house now 24/7. He would find a time everyday to call me though, but I never knew when that time would be… or if it would be the last time we ever talked. It was an emotionally grueling time for me… to not be able to be near him physically… to not be able to call him, or even know when and if he would call me. I kept my phone close by my side at all times and didn't do anything that would require me to turn off my phone… even during the yoga classes I taught I would let my students know that I may need to leave if I get a call that I was waiting for. I was a nervous wreck, I felt weak, emotionally beaten up and helpless. My focus was my phone and when would Matthew call and making sure I didn't miss that opportunity. He called me everyday and no one else. He was faithful and devoted to the very end. He would gather whatever energy he had to talk to me and he was always cheerful and positive.

Sometimes I would sit across the street and look out across at his bedroom window thinking that he was in that room and somehow that would make me feel closer to him. Then I thought of an idea to help us connect more throughout the day. I decided that I would send him his favorite flowers. I would use a code name (because they would have thrown them away if they knew they were from me), and I would hide stuff in the plant. I hid a sachet between the plant and the fancy pot it was put in. The first one I had sent from an orchid nursery so it was a bit tricky and nervous hiding the loot without anyone seeing me. But it worked and when he called that day I told him when it would be coming, what the code name would be, and where the gift sachet would be hidden. He called and was overjoyed when he found the hidden sachet filled with a heart shaped rock, a love note, kisses and hugs, and a picture of us up at our sacred cabin.

Once I figured that out and it worked, I was on a roll. I sent another plant with a love note and fun trinkets of love and affection for him to enjoy, I sent a smiley face cake, and a bunch of balloons… it became fun to think of what I could send to him next that he would enjoy. It was a way we could be together… a way I could send my energy and love to him in the only form I had available. The flowers and gifts became my proxy, they sat by his side when I couldn't and I found creative ways to tell him how much I loved him. My favorite gift was a small pine tree that represented our sacred cabin in the woods… our favorite spot in all the universe. The universe was so kind to me to help me find all the perfect decorations to make this tree the perfect symbol for our special heaven where we had shared so much love and held so many dear memories. I found a perfect rock to represent our kissing rock, I found a tiny toy moose with a bobbling head to represent the yearling moose that came by almost everyday that last year. I found a tiny toy squirrel and even a miniature silver balloon. I buried something underneath each decoration for him to find, a love note, a kiss, a smile, a heart, a poem.

When we talked that day I told him it would be coming the next day. I met a private courier person at a gas station parking lot and they delivered it to his home.

When we talked the next day he hadn't received the tree yet, but we had a few moments to tell one another how much we loved the other, and the call as usual was short but very sweet. The next day when he called I asked if he had received the tree and he got frustrated and snapped "no". We finished our call by saying, "I love you", but it wasn't our best call and I felt an incompletion… a sense of separation that burdened my heart. Our time to lovingly connect by phone was limited to only a few minutes… love was the only important thing to share. When we hung up I felt a sadness I had never known, I couldn't call him back, I couldn't go over to see him, I felt trapped and lost. The yearning to connect was overwhelming, I didn't know when he'd call again, and there was nothing I could do… I just sat and cried like a baby. Somewhere in the middle of my cries I heard the phone ring and to my enormous surprise it was Matthew. He called to apologize for getting upset and that he just wanted to tell me how much he loved me. I poured out my love for him, we poured out our hearts and shared such enormous warmth and love… we could feel the powerful oneness of our souls… we basked in the overwhelming rapture of our combined love. Both of our hearts were exploding with love and affection for the other, it was a perfect connection.

I am so deeply grateful that Matthew had called back that night because he never called again… that was our last phone call. He lived two more days and peacefully passed in his sleep one cold day in January of 2008.

Channeling France

$\mathscr{I}$t took you many years to get over the grief of losing me and you never really did. You and became great friends with Atkinson, who gradually grew into a man. He helped you with everything, he was very loyal to you and he always loved you. The two of you continued to travel together and you eventually found a place where you both felt at home… it was a beautiful wooded area that was not very populated. You always felt safe in the forest, and this area was heavily forested with the ocean not too far away.

You still thought of me constantly, even as the years passed… you always felt someday we would find one another again. You remained friends with Atkinson, and he never gave up on his dreams of being with you either. You grew to love Atkinson deeply, however your heart yearned and grieved for me. Eventually after nine years and several marriage proposals Atkinson gave up on you and moved away to follow his dreams in a nearby city.

I was a slave for a few years but all the men that were captured were freed during a raid. Once I was free I knew that I had to find you. I searched for years and finally settled into a populated area on the ocean and become a doctor. I wanted to learn everything about becoming a doctor… I wanted to find secrets… things no one knew about the human body yet.

At this time there weren't many answers for doctors but I was trying to develop some of my own ideas. One of my ideas happened when someone came in to get medical attention and her leg was broken. As I tried to help this patient, I stared at her leg and for a brief second I felt like I had seen through the leg. Now, of course, seeing through the leg was impossible at this time, even with a machine… but I saw it… I saw where the break was. I saw how the bone was out of alignment.

I helped to fix the patient's leg but could not explain what had happened with my vision. I told a few people what I had seen… they didn't believe me. I tried to figure out what had occurred to cause me to see the bone. Was it something I did? Was there some kind of reflection off of something from the sun? Most importantly, could I do it again and could others see through the leg also?

I was on a quest… I spent many, many days going to different towns and talking to anyone with any medical knowledge that would talk to me. As I was on my search for information, I also searched for you everywhere I went. I couldn't forget your face… it was etched in my mind and heart.

You began doing spiritual healing work… you lived in a small cabin deep in the woods and kept your work very private due to several doctors who questioned and even threatened you for what you were doing. However, you were healing and helping many people with your natural gift of healing. The news of your healing gift spread by word of mouth from the people you had helped. You never forgot about me and you never gave up hope that someday we would again find one another.

In one particular town when I was talking to a doctor I saw a women walk by very quickly and then disappear behind a building. I did not see her face but the way she moved reminded me of you… so without explaining to the doctor I ran after the woman. My eyes searched for the woman but I couldn't find her anywhere… it was like she just vanished in thin air. I was determined to stay in this town longer and find the woman that I thought may have been you. This was a very large town… more like a city. I continued to talk to every doctor or medical expert and all the while I looked for you… every spare moment I searched for you.

I walked up and down streets, frequented every possible establishment I thought you might visit. I searched every market place…especially the area I thought I had first seen you disappear behind the building.

While I was visiting this town searching for you, I had heard about a doctor who had a very large practice and was very well loved and respected in this city. He and I became very good friends… we spent a lot of time together… he showed me places in the area. When he had free time away from his practice he took me to a large river miles away from the city near a forest. It was warm so we would swim in the river and rest on the grassy banks and talk. We often would share about our lives… but I was more secretive of my past than he… I only shared the years after we separated… the years of becoming a doctor. One time however, we talked about women… he had told me about a woman he loved whom he tried for years to get her to marry him, but she was in love with another man. I felt safe with him for some reason and I shared how I had met my one true love but that circumstances happened that separated us, but how I never stopped loving her. Neither of us had any idea we were talking about the same woman. My friend was Atkinson.

I spent nine months in this area searching for you and finally gave up and made plans to go back to where my original practice was. Atkinson told me about a retired doctor that taught to from time to time… he told me that I should go talk to him before I leave… he told me that he was a bit unorthodox in his methods. This retired doctor lived several miles out of town so I decided that on my way home I would pay him a visit.

When I met this retired doctor I was shocked… it was the same man, our angel that you and I had run into that led us along our journey so many years ago. His face was a little different but he was the same person. So many memories flooded through me… of you… our travels… our escape from our families… our journeys and all the miracles, challenges, and synchronicities along the way. It had been years since I had seen this angel guide and I never saw him alone… we had always met him when we were together.

He smiled at me and without saying a word he told me that he knew who I was. When he began speaking to me he told me that if you and I hadn't experienced being physically separated that neither of us would have discovered our full potential… that we needed time apart to discover our gifts because they seem to contradict or oppose one another. He explained how they don't have to oppose… how they can compliment and add once they are combined with wisdom.

He then told me I needed to see one more doctor… a witchdoctor who practiced spiritual healing. I was a bit resistant because I had heard some negative things about these kinds of people… but I trusted this man so I agreed. He told me that this witchdoctor lived several more miles out away from the city, so I would need to stay the night with him and leave first thing in the morning.

In the morning the man gave me directions and I followed several paths that led to a forest… I continued to followed several more paths through the forest, over streams, up hills and through more forest. It was a delightful walk and my mind was mesmerized by the magic and beauty of this forest. It seemed to distract me from the mixed feelings I had of meeting this witchdoctor.

Finally I could see the small cottage nestled in the woods, surrounded by trees, flowers, and a small stream passing through the front yard. I approached the cottage slowly not sure what kind of person I was to meet, but also felt pulled toward the cottage… both apprehensive and excited to meet this mystery witchdoctor. I knocked on the door and in the next moment you answered the door… our eyes met. We remained speechless and silent for a long time… our eyes just locked onto one another. Neither one of us had expected to see one another that day… we both had grown discouraged that we'd never see each other again… yet neither of us ever lost hope.

We embraced and it seemed forever before we let one another go. I spun you around and you laughed… we noticed that we had each aged a little but what we felt in our hearts from the moment we met was exactly the same. You invited me in and we sat down and began to talk… each one explaining our lives. I told you that I had loved no other and you told me that you too had never stopped loving me… that you too could never be with another. We both shared how although there were times we felt greatly discouraged… that deep down in our hearts we knew that somehow, someway our hearts would bring us back to one another. That just like how they brought us together when we first met in the woods long, long ago… they would bring us back together again.

Touched by an Angel

The day Matthew passed I woke up in the morning and hadn't known he had passed… I curled up in my bed and held my phone close to my heart waiting for his call. I eventually went out to feed the birds… my phone in my pocket. I felt different as I walked across the backyard, I felt more aware. I noticed that my surroundings had fallen into disarray… that I had neglected so much during this traumatic experience. It seemed I had let some housecleaning and yard work go, but I didn't ever neglect the birds… no matter how I was feeling I fed the bird's everyday. Feeding the birds reminded me of Matthew and how he loved to feed the birds and squirrels up at TL. I felt the birds gave much more to me than I did for them… I simply gave them some food everyday and in return they filled my yard with their joyous songs, they put on a dance performance for me everyday, and they planted sunflowers for me to enjoy.

It wasn't until later that day when I found out that Matthew had passed and even though I had time to prepare and I knew it was inevitable, the news struck enormous grief through my heart and I curled up in bed and cried for days.

I was unable to go to his funeral because the family requested I not be present… but I was able to have my own funeral for Matthew up at TL, and many of our friends attended.

After Matthew had left I was unable to eat, I had no appetite and actually felt sick to my stomach most of the time. There was a peanut butter health bar I found at the health food store that was the only thing I was able to get down. People were getting a bit nervous because I was losing weight and had become a recluse, but I couldn't stomach any other food except that peanut butter health bar. I still taught my classes and continued my business but I had to force myself to do it and I didn't feel any energy to go out or do anything else.

From the day Matthew passed I dreamt of him at night… I loved my Matthew dreams because in my dreams it was as if Matthew was still alive. My first few dreams were unbelievably exhilarating because when he appeared in the dream I believed that he hadn't died. He would appear in a dream and I would say to him how I thought he had passed and how ecstatic I am that I was wrong, that he is still really alive, I would be filled with euphoria that he was there… that he was still alive… those dreams seemed so real. I looked forward to those dreams and knew when I had them that he was truly visiting me.

One night a month and a half after Matthew had passed I woke up at five am and couldn't get back to sleep. I was deeply sad and lonely… I missed Matthew so much. As I lay there all of a sudden I felt an energy surround me and embrace me very tightly. It felt so comforting, nurturing, and warm… like the juiciest, safest, most delicious and tight hug you could ever imagine. I had been so tense, so sad, and so devastated for so long that I allowed myself to indulge completely in the glowing warmth of this energetic embrace. It was as if my entire body was embraced, it was blissful, it was the first time I had felt any peace or relaxation since Matthew had gotten sick. I eventually fell back to sleep in the arms of this all-loving, full body hug. When I woke up I remembered the blissful experience and knew it was real and it was Matthew visiting me, but this time not in a dream but energetically to give me a hug.

I walked into the kitchen and opened the refrigerator and thought how I'd love to have some eggs for breakfast. Then I thought, 'Oh my goodness I want to eat, this is a miracle, I am actually hungry… I have my appetite back.' I thought about the hug early that morning and I knew somehow that Matthew had come not only to give me an incredibly loving hug, but to also heal me from some of the overwhelming grief that had taken my appetite.

It was painful to lose someone that was such a deep love… such a profoundly close soul connection and eternal friend. It was the most painful thing I had ever endured until then. But I would never take a moment back… both loving and losing Matthew has been a gift in my life… it has made me a stronger, wiser, and more compassionate person.

Before Matthew I was careful and guarded… I didn't allow myself to get close to too many people… I didn't feel safe and I didn't want to get hurt. You have a choice when you lose someone you are deeply and profoundly in love with… you can become bitter and closed down or you can allow yourself to open you up and become more vulnerable and fully alive. I consciously allowed the experience to open me up because I knew that was what Matthew would have wanted. I allowed it to teach me that nothing can destroy me… that I am stronger than anything that can ever happen to me. The overwhelming grief and pain of losing such a profound love hadn't killed me… the grief hadn't destroyed me… I was still alive and ok…I am still me. I also learned that death cannot destroy love… that Matthew has never really left me because I feel him everyday… he lives in my heart and is deeply connected to my soul. In some ways we are more connected now, we have an even more intimate relationship. I have not lost Matthew and I can never lose Matthew, or anyone else I love… love is far more powerful than anything in the physical world.

In time I have become stronger because I can love more deeply, I don't have to protect myself and fear intimacy. I can love people deeply and profoundly and allow them to touch and bless my life as Matthew did.

Matthew gave me thousands of gifts by entering my life… he taught me how to think outside the box… he taught me how to give truly… he taught me how to see the good in everyone and everything… he helped me open up to my creativity… he taught me what true forgiveness is… he helped me financially… he showed me how life is much more than what the five senses can perceive… he brought me a joy and a sense of safety in the world I had never known. He brought humor, magic, ingenuity, kindness, thoughtfulness, and wonderment into my life. He loved me unconditionally in a way I had never known or experienced with anyone in my life. He loved me with all my strengths and weaknesses, he loved me through the good and the bad, he loved me unceasingly, deeply, uniquely in a way that transformed my heart and soul deep down to the very core of my being. His unending love healed and transformed me and to this very day continues to heal and transform me. He taught me what love means and how to truly love another…through his death he taught me how to live.

Matthew taught me that it is never the "things" in life that make a difference but the relationships, the love, and the experiences we get to share with others that is most important and fulfilling. Another person's presence in our life is what makes us wealthy… the loving connections we experience with others are what brings us true and lasting joy. Matthew taught me to love, value, and appreciate all the relationships in my life. Every physical person in our life will someday be gone, but the love that we shared with one another will remain forever within our hearts… true love is the only thing in all the universe that is eternal.

The End